Hours later, Jessie and Meredith sprawled out on sleeping bags in the middle of the bedroom floor. Moonlight streamed in through an open window, bathing their naked bodies. Somewhere in the distance, a hound brayed mournfully at the moon, the sound so eerie it sent cold chills through Meredith, making her shiver.

"This is the first time I've felt safe since I saw those men," Meredith said. "God! Finally a place we can call our own. It feels wonderful even without electricity and plumbing!" She snuggled so the length of her body fit perfectly with the ins and outs of Jessie's.

"I've never felt anything as wonderful as your body," Jessie whispered. "Who could have known that anything could feel like this?"

"Remember when we used to wrestle with each other when we were kids?" Meredith laughed softly. "I loved touching you then. I used to deliberately pick arguments with you, so you would finally grab me and we would roll around on the ground, fighting."

"You really are bad," Jessie said, gazing at her face in wonder. "You never told me that. I thought you hated me then." She stroked Meredith's cool smooth cheek, then traced the outline of her eyes and shell-like ears with gentle fingers. Slowly and deliberately, she ran her tongue along the curves of Meredith's body, moving downward . . .

The Chesapeake Project

PHYLLIS HORN

The Chesapeake Project

PHYLLIS HORN

The Naiad Press, Inc.
1990

Printed in the United States of America
First Edition

Edited by Ann Klauda
Cover design by Pat Tong and Bonnie Liss
    (Phoenix Graphics)
Typeset by Sandi Stancil

Library of Congress Cataloging-in-Publication Data

Horn, Phyllis, 1938—
    The Chesapeake project / by Phyllis Horn.
        p.   cm.
    ISBN 0-941483-58-4
    I. Title.
PS3558.0686C49   1990
813'.54--dc20   89-48967
                                                          CIP

About the Author

Phyllis Horn claims her soul was born when she moved to the banks of the Chesapeake Bay with her life partner. She spends most of the year disguised as a member of the faculty of a large eastern university, but her real self emerges during the summer months when she has the time to write and fish and crab. This is her first novel.

To Lady Di
who taught me how to love
and be loved.

With Thanks

To Jane, who once again blazed a trail. My thanks and love.

To Becky Ellis, whose early encouragement kept me writing.

To Cassie, my toy poodle, who sat at my feet from the first word to the last.

And to all the rest of you who didn't laugh when I said I was writing a novel.

Chapter One

1

Sybil's Bar and Grill was located on an isolated stretch of Highway 5 that ran parallel to the Potomac River. Beside the bar, a metal trailer housed the Post Office for the town of Pliney Point, Maryland. The town, if indeed you could call it a town, had a population of about four hundred. The next closest thing to civilization was the county seat, twelve miles away.

Nearly all the men in the area worked the water

for a living, pulling in crab pots in the summer and oystering or dredging for crabs in the winter. For the most part, the women kept house for the men, and the kids escaped to nearby Washington or Baltimore when they were able to raise the twenty-five dollars for bus fare.

As soon as it was dark, especially when the summer reruns took over the TV, the local watermen congregated at Sybil's to swap tales and drink beer. This night in early May was no different.

"Life don't get no sweeter than when the bay's full of crabs like it is now," Clarence Owens said to his crabbing partner, Tommy Moon. He rolled a can of Budweiser between his calloused hands as he spoke. "My granddaddy said there was a time when you could just go along in an ol' dinghy and scoop the mothers off the top of the water with a net. Didn't need no crab pots and fancy equipment. Just go pick 'em off the water like picking fruit out of the trees."

Moon leaned forward on the drink-stained table and raised his beer glass in a toast to Owens. They had come in the bar together after dinner for a night of hard drinking and bragging. "We made us a mint today, we did! Me and Clarence gonna be rich before oyster season," he said loud enough for the half-dozen other crabbers in the bar to hear.

"They ain't gonna be any more good times like your grandpa talked about, Clarence," Kenny Westerlake said. "Crabs are mostly gone from the Chesapeake Bay. Oysters too. Too much crap from the cities being dumped into it."

"Shit, man, you're just like most other watermen. Too damn lazy to make a good living off the water.

2

You have to work hard at it. Me and Tommy was haulin' in crab pots by four-thirty this morning and nobody'd seen your ugly butt yet." Owens pulled up his ratty white T-shirt and scratched the black curly hair on his beer-swollen stomach. He leaned back in his chair and stuck out his chin, daring anybody to disagree with him. Owens loved nothing better than a good fight.

"Tell you what, boys," Sybil Ekstrand, the bar's owner broke in as she touched the large plate glass window at the front of the building. "If you'll kiss and make up before this argument gets into high gear, I'll buy you all another beer. I don't want to replace this window again because of your fighting. I've done it three times already in the last year!"

"I'll serve it up if you're buying," Kenny Westerlake volunteered, and headed for the bar. He moved with the easy swagger of a waterman, pushing his sun-bleached hair back from his eyes as he walked. He wore dirty rubber boots over faded jeans like all the other men in Sybil's, but his chambray shirt was clean and crisp looking. "Don't worry," he said to Sybil quietly, "I'll make 'em keep a lid on it tonight. You don't have to stand in front of the window to protect it."

Sybil smoothed back a stray strand of her red hair. The rubber band she used on her pony tail never seemed to hold it all. She smiled at Kenny to show her gratitude for his concern. "Well, this place is all I've got, and it just kills me to see those apes wreck it, God love 'em."

"Looks like your clientele is improving," Kenny remarked as the bell over the front door tinkled. He nodded in the direction of a tall girl with long

3

chestnut hair that fell to the waist of her jeans. Her face was oval with a strong cleft chin. She had prominent cheekbones, suggestive of Indian ancestry, and a clean jaw line. Her face was free of make-up, the skin without blemish and burnished to a deep coppery tan.

"Hi, Sybil." The girl's voice was deep and resonant. Her eyes searched the cafe as she spoke.

"Hi, yourself, Jessie. How you doing? Guess you're working hard these days with crab season moving into full swing." Sybil reached out and tugged playfully at the sweatshirt Jessica Andrews wore, charcoal gray with red letters that said University of Maryland.

Jessie raised her broad shoulders in a shrug. "You know me. Never have thought crabbing was work. I love it too much. You haven't seen my daddy this evening, have you?"

"No, honey, haven't seen him in a couple of days. You know he never comes in here unless it's to pick up a loaf of bread or something."

Jessie looked around the room again as if she might find him there no matter what Sybil said. She stuffed her large hands into her jeans pockets and exhaled a quiet sigh.

"You all right, Jessie?"

"Yeah, I'm fine. It's just that — it's gettin' dark and I don't know where Dad is. I've been looking all over for him. He had some errands to run this afternoon but he's always home for supper around five o'clock no matter what. He hasn't shown up this evening. Your place was sort of the last resort. Thought he might have come in here."

4

Sybil looked at her with motherly concern. "Maybe some of the other crabbers have seen him." She yelled in the direction of Moon and Owens. "Any of you fellows seen Andy Andrews lately?"

"He was down at the Selvey's Wharf this morning. Ain't seen him since though," Owens said. "He thinks he's too damned good to hang around with the likes of us after work, don't you know."

"Sorry, Jess," Sybil said. "If he does come by here I'll tell him to call you. Tell him you're looking for him, okay? I expect he just got to talking with somebody and forgot the time. I wouldn't worry." She started toward the bar, then turned back. "How's your friend Meredith? Haven't seen her in a month of Sundays."

"About like always, I guess. I'll tell her you asked."

2

Sybil watched as Jessie walked with long strides out to the old blue Pontiac that she and her father kept as a backup vehicle for their pickup truck. Even in the twilight, Sybil could see that the bottoms of the doors and fenders were rusted through, victims of long exposure to salt spray and sea air.

"That old car's sure seen better days," Sybil mused to herself. "Like this place." She examined the cafe with a critical eye. It seemed seedy-looking and run down. Maybe it was time to put a little money into paint and new tables.

"Kenny," she said, as he walked up behind her

5

and put his hands lightly on her shoulders, "you think I ought to fix this place up? Might help business."

"I don't know why you'd want to go and do that. We just got it broke in good from the last time you fixed it up. Besides that," he added with a flourish, "*you* don't have to worry about business! You sell the best, I say, the very best, hamburgers and beer for miles around!"

"I sell the *only* hamburgers and beer for miles around, you idiot!" She crossed her arms over her ample bosom.

"Anyway, if you'd marry me it wouldn't matter —"

She held up her hand to stop him. "Don't start that again, Kenny! I've told you a hundred times you're a sweet guy, but I'll take a life of selling beer and burgers *any day* to being married to a waterman. I tried that twice! You're all too wild for me!"

Kenny was about to protest when a soul-searing screech of rubber tires on cement made him look up. "Godalmighty, get a load of that," he breathed as he looked over Sybil's head through the window.

The Ford Escort was still swaying on its springs when the driver stumbled out of the car and stiff-armed the front door, scattering a display of Fritos and Cheetos all over the floor. His chin and forehead were chalky white but his cheeks were dayglow red.

A shocked silence hung over the room until Clarence Owens exclaimed drunkenly, "Christ on a crutch! Where the hell's the fire, stranger?"

6

The man looked around with glazed eyes. Over and over he ran his fingers through his straight dark hair. He was gulping air and there was a string of spit running out of his mouth down across his chin.

"I was — I was — I was, uh —" he intoned incoherently.

Sybil put her hand on the back of his jacket and pushed his overweight body in the direction of an empty chair. "Please, do sit down! Kenny, maybe you should call the rescue squad."

As the man collapsed into the chair, he took a deep shuddering breath, then shook himself like a wet dog. His color began to return slowly. "Don't call the rescue squad," he told them. "But you better call the sheriff."

Kenny stared blankly at Sybil, not sure what to do next.

"Listen," the man said, talking fast. "I'm a salesman. Name's McFarland. From Waldorf. I'm heading home, see, and I spot this old church down the road. Looks like to me it's a good place to stop and, ah, take a leak, you know."

Moon said suspiciously, "What you want the sheriff for?"

"There's been a murder! There's a dead body down by that church." The blood began draining down from his face again. "And he don't have no eyes!" McFarland's own eyes grew big and bright.

"What do you mean, no eyes? Everybody's got eyes," Owens said with a funny little sneer in his voice. His upper lip rolled up over his tobacco-stained teeth.

"No eyes, is what I mean! At least not where eyes are supposed to be!" McFarland answered.

"Not where they're supposed to be?" Sybil echoed tentatively. Her insides were beginning to contract.

"Not unless they was supposed to be in his mouth. Stuck in between his teeth, they were, and looking right up at me!"

Sybil's Bar and Grill emptied quickly as the men hit the front door together and on the run. A chorus of pickup truck engines droned out into the night.

3

"Jerry, just take the body on over to the hospital morgue," Sheriff Todd said to the driver of the Volunteer Rescue Squad vehicle. "These people don't need to see any more of this horror show. They've had enough excitement for one night."

"That's for sure," Jerry Hudgins agreed, straightening the back of his white laundry-starched lab coat. He was trying to appear very businesslike, as if this were old hat to him, and it irritated him greatly that he couldn't stop looking at the mutilated body.

A regular pickup truck caravan had come from Sybil's, everybody eager to get a look at the grisly corpse. Sybil had called the county sheriff's office and her Aunt Bess before she'd locked up the store and made tracks like everybody else to the church yard. Aunt Bess, so it seemed, had called all the people in her neighborhood and they'd called their friends. Now the church yard looked a lot like the high school football field in July during the 4-H competition.

8

The rescue squad driver and his aide lifted the dead man onto the gurney, covered him with a blanket and tightened the straps. "Don't want him to get up and walk away," the aide said and laughed nervously as he closed the van door.

"Everybody get the hell out of the way! Move it now," the driver yelled with pompous authority at the crush of curious people. He shouldered his way to the front of the vehicle and climbed in. He hit the siren to clear a path and turned on the dome light. It scattered pulsating blood-red light across the church yard.

"What you think happened to him, Sheriff?" Clarence Owens asked in a bewildered tone. He was cold sober after looking at the body.

"Somebody killed him, that's what I think. A man don't usually choke on his own eyes. You think something different, Owens?" Sheriff Todd didn't care much for Owens. He had wasted too many Saturday nights trying to keep him from getting killed in drunken fights.

"You know him, don't you?" Owens asked.

"Sure. Don't you?"

"You bet. Andy Andrews. Been fishing alongside of him most of my life, I guess. Worked for him once. A hard ass if I ever saw one. Ain't nobody 'round here liked him much."

"Haven't seen his daughter, have you?" the sheriff asked without enthusiasm. No matter how often he had done it, he dreaded talking to a victim's relatives.

"She's over there with Sybil," Owens replied. "Somebody called her when they saw it was her daddy. She come on out here. Don't know as I'd trust much of what she says though, Sheriff. She's weird as her crazy ol' man, if you know what I mean. Hanging around that Tompkins gal all the time." He winked broadly at Todd as if sharing a well-kept secret.

Todd narrowed his blue-gray eyes. "Don't know anything about that. Know she's been working on her dad's boat since she was a little thing and her momma's been dead for years. She's gonna take this real hard." The sheriff abruptly walked away from Owens and made his way through the crowd.

A knot of people had gathered around Sybil and Jessie, but they moved quickly aside as Todd approached. He had noticed years before that people wouldn't touch him when he had his uniform on.

"Evening, Ms. Ekstrand. Ms. Andrews," Todd said politely, taking off his highway patrol hat.

"Sheriff Todd," Sybil said, acknowledging his greeting. She put a protective arm around Jessie as if the sheriff were somehow dangerous.

"Ms. Ekstrand. Sybil," Todd began tentatively. "I *have* to talk to Jessie about this."

"Seems kind of heartless to do it right now," Sybil protested, giving him a reproachful look.

A shiver ran through Jessie's body as the chilly night breeze blew in little crazy circles that cut to the bone. She pulled her green and brown camouflage-style fatigue jacket tight to her body. Dimly, muffled by the distance, the ambulance siren whined above the murmurs of the crowd.

"What you want me to tell you, Sheriff?" Jessie said. "I thought it was your job to find out what happened."

10

Something in her tone stabbed at Todd's insides. "I am sorry," he replied gently. "I know how terrible this must be for you." He looked down at his spit-polished boots and studied them for a few seconds. "I guess it goes without saying this was no accident. If you know something, anything at all . . . I'll do everything I can."

"Looks like to me there's not much you can do," she said, "unless you think you can bring him back from the dead." A look of agony passed through her eyes and settled on her mouth. She sucked in her breath with a near sob that jerked the corners of her mouth down until it seemed she might cry out.

"Sheriff Todd, really!" Sybil protested. "Do you have to do this now?"

Todd sighed, the way a man will sigh from extreme fatigue. "You shouldn't have come out here, Jessie. Whoever called you shouldn't have." It crossed his mind that often people could be exceptionally cruel under the guise of helpfulness. "Let me drive you home. Maybe we can talk a little on the way if you feel like it."

"I can drive myself home, thanks. But if you think you need to talk to me, we can do that."

4

As Todd and Jessie walked away from Sybil across the church parking lot, the clamor of automotive engines beat on their ear drums. The show was over now that the body was gone. Everybody was ready to get on back home. Or back to serious beer drinking.

11

As she reached the car, Jessie pulled a handkerchief out of her back pocket and made a feeble swipe at her nose. "I don't know what I can tell you, Sheriff. You know more than I do. He must have told you what was going on when he came to your office to talk to you this morning."

Todd leaned heavily against the squad car and raised his eyebrows. "I don't know anything, Jessie. I haven't seen your father in over a week."

"What? But he said —" She went stiff with surprise, trying to absorb the information.

"Said he was coming to see me?" he anticipated. "Then somebody stopped him before he got there."

"Listen," Jessie said. Then paradoxically said nothing.

Todd pitched his hat through the open window of the squad car and wiped his sweaty palms over the rough fabric of his dark wool Eisenhower jacket. "Let's get in the squad car," he told her.

Jessie drew her lanky body up tightly as she got into the passenger's seat. In the moonlight, Todd could see her clench and unclench her jaw.

"Was your daddy in any kind of trouble?" he asked, knowing full well that she might not tell him even if she knew. Watermen and their families were a secretive bunch who figured their own business was their own business, good or bad.

"Maybe so, but what difference can it make now?" she replied wearily. "He's dead. Nothing I say can make the slightest bit of difference."

Todd studied her face in the moonlight. A look of horror sat behind her eyes. She looked far older than her twenty-one years. He shook his head, then said gently, "You're right. I can't bring him back. But I

12

can try to find whoever did this. Find out *why* this happened. Don't you want whoever did it to be punished?"

Jessie shrugged. "I'm not sure if I want that or not," she said in a level tone. "If he was in trouble bad enough that somebody would kill him, I'm not sure I want to know what it was."

"If he was mixed up in something bad enough for somebody to commit murder, Jessie, I have to find out about it. Other people — even you — may be in danger. Somebody may think he told you what he was coming to tell me."

A look of surprise crossed her face. The shock of her father's death had kept her from thinking beyond the moment. "Are you serious, Sheriff? Somebody might come after me?"

"There's a chance that might be the case. But for chrissake don't worry. I'll put you under protective custody. I can keep someone with you round the clock."

Jessie looked him resolutely in the eye. She didn't want some nosy watchdog hanging around, especially when she was with Meredith. They had little enough privacy as it was. "Sheriff, I don't mean to sound ungrateful, but I can take care of myself." She set her chin stubbornly.

"Nobody can take care of themselves against someone who'd commit this kind of crime, Jessica. It's my job to see nothing happens to you."

"Sheriff, you know something? You wouldn't be trying so hard to protect me if I was a man. But I can take care of myself. I don't need a bodyguard, believe me. Nobody can work the water like I do and not be as strong as an ox."

13

He stared into her eyes for a moment. He knew he wouldn't assign a deputy to watch out for a man. Not yet anyway. He also knew that most of the women who lived in this part of Maryland were not like the women he had known in Baltimore, where he came from. They seemed stronger somehow, and more self-sufficient.

"Okay," he said, but felt a touch of irritation for giving in to her so easily. "Okay. Okay. I won't assign anybody to you. That is, unless someone tries to hurt you. Then all bets are off. Agreed?"

She relaxed a little. "Agreed. But I don't know much to tell you."

"What was *he* coming to tell me, Jessie?" he prompted her.

"I don't know exactly," she began with hesitation, "but something unusual did happen. Maybe it's important. Maybe not."

She stared out into the darkness. It had been just last night but it seemed like a thousand years ago. She replayed the whole scene again from inside her head before she spoke. Rushing back from being with Meredith. Jogging across the corn fields that separated their two houses. Then seeing the car in the driveway. She had stopped at the end of the woods to try to catch her breath, to make herself look composed when she went into the house. Two men walked out of the house just as she got there. One was big. Fat. The other was a skinny little man. When they had gotten into the car to leave, the tires had spun so hard they left tracks in the dirt driveway.

She told Todd about it. Everything except being with Meredith. "It was a dark-colored car. I couldn't

14

see what color exactly. A Buick, I think. A big car for sure. I think those men saw me in the headlights when they drove away. I asked Dad about it but he wouldn't say much. Just that they had come to see him on some business. But he looked so awful, Sheriff, I knew something pretty bad had happened. He looked almost sick. Then today he said he was going to drop by to see you. He didn't tell me what for, but I figured he was going to tell you something about those men. Christ, they must have been watching him. And stopped him before he could —"

She held her breath for a few seconds, imagining what must have happened. "Jesus!" she said, hugging her long arms to her chest. "I should have gone with him!"

"You mustn't blame yourself, Jessie," Todd said evenly. "He wouldn't have wanted to put you in any danger. He must have known something bad might happen."

"I know he wouldn't," she said. "Guess he would have thought of me as his little girl if I'd been sixty years old." Ironically, she laughed.

Before he could reply, she opened the door and got out of the car. "Thanks a lot for your concern, Sheriff, but I have a lot of things to do. You just let me know if you find out something else."

5

Hours later Jessie stood at the edge of the woods that surrounded the Tompkins house, watching the lacy curtains at Meredith's bedroom window flutter in the cool spring breeze. Light from a full moon trickled through the tall pine trees, making the night sparkle as if the world were a Walt Disney movie and magic elves might appear to sing and dance in a circle. Only there was no singing; just the dead silence of the rural countryside ringing in her ears.

Her thoughts drifted unbidden back to the evening before. "Do you want to make love tonight? Out here in the woods?" Meredith had asked as they walked hand in hand down a familiar path.

Surprised, she replied, "Do you really want to? You're always saying how much you hate it because we don't have a bed of our own to make love in."

"Don't you know I *want* to make love every time we're together, Jess? And besides, it wouldn't be the first time we've done it in the woods, now would it?" Meredith teased. "We can go down by that old deserted mill house again. Nobody ever comes down there."

Jessie remembered the pungent smell of the pine needles and the musky leaves as they lay down, using their clothes for a ground cover. Meredith's hands running lovingly up and down Jessie's strong, muscular body. Then Jessie shuddered and nearly gasped as knowing fingers slid lightly over and over the places of her sensitive secrets.

Jessie held her close for a long time, then took her mouth to Meredith's breasts and tenderly circled each pink nipple slowly with her tongue until it stood erect. Gently, she kissed her eyes and nose. Then she began a trail of tiny kisses down the inside of her arm.

"I want you, want you, want you, Jessie! Please hurry!" Meredith said hoarsely. Her teeth bit possessively into Jessie's neck until Jessie pulled free,

16

capturing Meredith's mouth with her own until the demanding tongue and lips melted into sensuous tenderness.

"Go slow, baby," Jessie whispered. "Take your time. You don't have to be afraid. Nobody's coming down here. You're going to hurry the best of your life away."

"I'm not afraid. Put your hand here." Meredith cupped Jessie's long fingers between her legs. She slid her arms around Jessie's hips and pulled her tightly to her, beginning a slow deep grind.

"Easy, Meredith," Jessie had told her. "There's time and time again for all the love you want . . ."

The irony of those words came back now as Jessie walked silently to the window on the first floor of the old weather-worn house, watching for any sign of life. Her hands were cold and she pushed them deep into the pockets of her jacket. She shivered, not from the cold but from the thought of what she was going to tell Meredith. She would tell her that their time had run out.

"Meredith," she called in a whisper, through the open window. "Meredith, it's me. Jessie." She struck a match and held it high so the light would fall on her face.

"Jessie? Jessie, what are you doing? It's late. It must be after midnight." The voice was soft and husky with sleep.

Jessie reached up for the window screen. Quietly she worked it loose and dropped it quickly to the ground. "I'm coming in. I have to talk to you."

Meredith shook her blonde hair out of her face and moved sluggishly toward the window. She was not tall, only five-three or -four, but her legs were

17

long and coltish. Her high, firm breasts made her look mature, and older than her twenty years. The hands that reached for Jessie were delicate and slender. "Let me help you. What are you doing over here this time of night?"

Jessie climbed over the threshold of the window and dropped silently to the floor, her movements light, like a cat's. "I can't stay long, but I had to talk to you tonight. I had to tell you — my daddy's dead, Meredith," she said, her throat constricting so that she almost choked. "I don't guess you heard."

"Oh, my God! No, I hadn't heard. I went to bed early. Oh Jessie!" Meredith moved at once into her arms. For a time they held each other in the darkness.

Jessie abruptly broke away. She stared solemnly into Meredith's upturned face in the moonlight, taking in the sweetness of the eyes, the soft mouth that she loved so much. "I just had to see you, Meredith. I think I'm in a lot of danger."

"Danger? What on earth are you talking about? Why would you be in danger?" She pulled her thin pajamas tight around her chest against the night's chill.

"Because of my daddy. Somebody — God, Meredith, somebody *murdered* him. I don't know what he'd gotten himself involved in, but some strange men came to the house last night after I was with you. They saw me. I'm afraid they'll think I know something and they're going to be after me too." She hesitated, then went on. "I've been thinking we shouldn't see each other for a while. That way *you'll* be safe at least."

Meredith took her by the shoulders and looked into her dark sad eyes. "Jess, wait a minute. You're not thinking clearly. What could they think you know?"

"They surely believe I know who they are. I saw them. I don't know what else they might think besides that. But Meredith, there's no way of knowing what might happen." Spasms shook her, taking possession of her whole body. The tears started to come, but she wouldn't let them fall. She felt sick with loss and fear.

"My God, sweetheart. My God!" Meredith held her shoulders tightly. "Jessie, this is awful about your father, but there's no way we're not going to see each other."

"We can't, Meredith. It's too dangerous. I can face them, but I don't want you hurt because of me." She focused her eyes on the floor, avoiding Meredith's eyes.

"Jess, I love you. You don't think you can just stop seeing me just like that, do you? We've been planning to live together when the time was right. Jessie, this is the right time. I can move in with you now. Why can't you see this is the perfect opportunity?" She half-turned away. Her eyes glistened with tears in the moonlight.

Jessie sighed deeply, such a sigh of defeat and despair that she shuddered from it. "You don't know it all, Meredith. I think they sent me a message not to tell what I saw. When they killed him . . . they

19

. . . they cut out his eyes. Oh sweet Jesus, I can't stand to think about it!" Her whole body sagged on the bed at once, like a marionette whose strings had suddenly been cut. She sobbed long racking sobs into Meredith's bedspread.

Meredith reached for her, stroking her thick hair and murmuring words of comfort. Gently, she slipped her arm behind Jessie's shoulders and lifted her until she looked straight into her eyes. "Oh Jess, my love. I'll help you get through this. I will!"

"Maybe we won't have to stay away from each other for more than a few months, I don't know."

Meredith stared at her. She drew a deep breath and when she spoke her voice took on a hard edge. "So what'll you do? Just pretend that I don't exist, after all we've been to each other and after all the promises we've made? Jessie, I don't give a royal fuck about trouble. We're in this thing together, no matter how bad things get."

"Meredith, I'm not going to put you in danger. It's okay for me. But you. I can't let you —"

"Let me what?" Meredith's voice was loud and her chest heaved. "Let me have a happy life with you? Let me love you? What makes you think you have the right to *let* me do anything? Don't you think I should have a say in this? Shit, Jessie! I'm tired of letting you make all the decisions. And I'm tired of waiting for the things I want."

Jessie smiled for the first time. "I didn't mean —"

"Yes, you did, dammit! Let me tell you something, girl," Meredith said, raising her voice further. "I may not be *quite* as old as you are, but nobody, not even you, *lets* me do anything."

From the other bedroom, a voice boomed. "Meredith? You watching that damned television this time of night? Turn it off and go to sleep! I mean it now!"

"Oh God, it's your dad! You woke him up yelling at me. If he's drunk he'll try to beat the life out of me for being over here so late. I gotta go!" Jessie gave her a quick kiss on the lips and headed for the window, leaping through it to the ground.

Meredith's head appeared over the sill. "I'm going to be with you, silly," she whispered loudly after her. "Don't you think you can get away from me that easily. I'm going to move in with you and we're going to live together. And we're going to face this thing together too, you hear? You hear?"

The muffled echo of Jessie's feet running through the pine needles was her only answer.

Chapter Two

1

The next morning, Jessie trudged along the path leading to the dock, the path crunchy under her feet as the broken oyster shells split, creating a popping sound with every step. Fog lifted from the water, making the air seem thick and colder than it really was.

The workboat, the *Annie-O,* named after her mother, was exactly as she and her father had left it the day before. She could still see her father's burly body, muscles straining under the weight of the baskets of blue crabs as he carried them from the pier to the pickup truck.

She thought of the last conversation she had had with him: "Jess, you stay here and get the boat cleaned up. Made a mess of her today, we did. Lots of crabs and lots of mud. Early crabs always muddy from spending the winter on the bottom of the bay," he had said. "I'll take 'em on up to Selvey's Wharf. Should get a good price."

She had nodded her agreement and waved.

"Then I'm gonna go into the sheriff's office at the courthouse before I come back," he had shouted out of the pickup window just before he pulled away. "Should be home on time though."

She had had the feeling that he had waited to tell her so that she wouldn't be able to go. "Hold on a minute! I want to go with you!" she had yelled. But the shiny black truck had gone up the dirt road without her.

Now she said aloud to herself, "You sweet old son of a bitch, why didn't you trust me enough to take me with you?"

At the age of ten she had become his right hand on the boat. She had believed he needed her. Her mother's death from cancer had left them both empty. Weekends and summers on the *Annie-O* had become theirs, and she absorbed all he knew about the cunning ways of the water creatures. She worked long and hard beside him — like a man, as the local people seemed compelled to add. And through the years, she had put aside most of her own life to make his a little better. Even when Meredith had pleaded with her to leave him to make a home with her.

"God, Meredith," she would say, "He's just like any other man. If I wasn't there to feed him, he'd starve to death."

Meredith claimed her attachment to him was neurotic, but Jessie just thought of it as love for the man who was her idol. But she loved Meredith too — ever since they were children walking to the bus stop. They had double-dated together in high school. Then suddenly, at the age of sixteen, Jessie realized that she had gone out with those boring obnoxious boys in order to be near Meredith. The awareness of those feelings had paralyzed her for months before she could bring herself to tell Meredith how she felt.

She ran her fingers over the hard and glossy white paint on the bow of the boat. It made her think of the firmness of her own body in contact with the softness of Meredith. That first night, when she had finally confessed her love, Meredith had smiled in evident self-satisfaction before she said, "Why did you wait so long to tell me? I've always known I loved you." She had kissed Jessie deeply and they had made love that first time with an instinctive knowing of female body for female body.

Even now, in spite of her sadness, the thought sent a funny, excited little chill shooting through her and Jessie smiled. It was a warm thought too, like being wrapped in a flannel blanket on a winter night.

"What you got to smile about?" a man's voice said, startling her out of her reverie. The man behind the voice moved out into the open where she could see him.

She drew in a quiet gasp before she recognized him. "That you, Owens?" Jessie asked guardedly. "Why don't you scare the living shit out of somebody?"

Clarence Owens stepped onto the boat and did a quick appraisal as if he were looking for something. A grin crossed his face above the wiry mat of hair sticking up from his dirty sweatshirt. "Some people got too much shit in 'em to scare it out all at once. Could be you're one of 'em. Know your daddy was," Owens answered, baiting her.

"You get off my boat if you came out here to run your filthy mouth about my daddy. It's not my fault he wouldn't have anything to do with a jackass like you. You're still pissed because he fired you, aren't you?"

"Rather I'd run my mouth about you and that little gal down the road? Kind of *queer*, ain't it, how you're always runnin' after her? Looking at her all moon-eyed? You one of them *funny* gals?"

"Just take yourself off my property, Owens," she managed to squeeze out with great control. Her eyes narrowed as she spoke. "Everybody in the county knows what an asshole you are. Always got to be starting something with somebody, haven't ya'?"

"Ain't your property as I know of," Clarence barked back. "Word has it it's the bank's property now. Gonna be repossessed, I expect. Don't think no bankman in his right mind is gonna make a loan to a water-working female. Ain't nobody would work for the likes of you, even if you *was* a man. Too much like your goddamned daddy. Always acting better than anybody else. I know you ain't though."

Jessie knew there was some truth to what he was

25

saying about her father. He had owed a lot of people money. And nobody would work for him. She remembered the arguments they had had over her teenage love for swearing. After her mother died, he didn't exactly get religion, but he never swore. He never drank again either, and he wouldn't allow it from anybody else on his boat. The other watermen thought it just wasn't worth the deprivation to work for him. One of the things she had liked best about her father was that he had always tried to do what he thought was right, stuck to whatever he thought was the best thing, with no self-serving compromises. Or at least that was what she *had* believed.

"What do you want from me, Owens?" she asked him directly. "I don't want to fight with you."

"Oh, just thought I might be able to do you a favor. Take your old man's no-account boat off your hands. You can't handle her by yourself. She's too damned big."

"What you planning to do with her if you think she's so no-account? Besides, you and Moon got a boat now." Jessie knew better than to trust the man. He'd cheat the devil if he thought he could get away with it.

"Well, a *man* who works the water can always use another boat. I'm pretty good at fixin' 'em up, you know," he said, looking full of confidence. "Just thought since you were probably a little hard up for money, I'd do you a good deed. Take her off your hands. I hear your daddy owed everybody in the county."

Jessie suddenly felt defeated and tired. He was probably right. The watermen around Pliney Point would think it was beneath them to work for a woman. The boat *was* large for one person to handle and she would need money. "And you're prepared to offer me a small fortune for her, I guess?"

Owens looked at his boots as if he was struggling with a decision. Then he stuffed his hands down deep into the pockets of his faded pants and made a show of jingling the coins he found there.

"Tell you what I'll do. Just as a favor to you, mind you. I'm gonna take that old tub off your hands. How does two thousand dollars sound to you?" He looked at her hard, as if daring her to challenge the offer.

"Like somebody picked my pocket," Jessie said, stepping onto the dock. With squared shoulders she headed up the path toward the house. "We just spent nearly that overhauling the engine."

Owens caught up with her and grabbed her sleeve, jerking her around to face him. His mocking laughter came from deep in his barrel chest. "Maybe you'll like livin' on a welfare check," he said, "but I don't think you gonna have much left over to buy presents for that pretty Tompkins gal. Better take any offer you can get, Madam Queen!"

Miserable little piss-ant, Jessie thought, and she glared at him as she jerked her arm away. "You listen to me, Owens. I don't know what you think you know and I don't give a shit. You just stay away from me, you hear? And keep your goddamned hands off my boat and off of me!"

Owens studied her face for a moment, trying to gauge the extent of her resilience. She was tougher than he thought she would be. "Okay, kid," he said, grinning a yellow-toothed grin. "I'll give you four thousand for her in cash. But I won't go one red cent over that."

"That's more like it. Let's go get the registration papers." Jessie turned and headed back to the house, leaving him standing.

2

Meredith came through the front door of her own house. Her shoes were damp with dew from her long walk in the woods. She had needed some time to think.

The smell of the house was awful. It hit her like a wave of fog rolling off the morning tide and made her nostrils flare so that she could almost feel her nose hairs stiffen. Kerosene burning in the stove laid the foundation for the male sweat-stench that seemed to have found its way into the very floors and walls of the house. Sometimes the sweaty smell combined with the smell of her father's vomit — depending on how much he had had to drink and how sick it had made him.

Her eyes burned from a sleepless night of worry. She sat down at the kitchen table, staring blankly at the pink and blue formica top. The sticky remains of runny egg yolks and jelly left on breakfast plates stared back. Her father and her three brothers had left long before dawn for the dock and a day of crabbing.

"Who's there? That you, Meredith?" The voice called from the back bedroom.

"It's me, Momma."

28

"Come in here, child," the voice from the back called again. Lately her mother's voice had begun to resemble her body, broken and bent and so weary that it seemed each word might be the last.

A strangled sob met Meredith as she moved to the door of her parents' bedroom. Carefully, she sat down on the edge of the bed. "Momma, what's the matter now?" she asked.

"Meredith, you'll have to clean up the kitchen. I just can't do it today. Please, honey, do it for me, won't you?"

The woman who lay on the bed could have been seventy instead of forty-five. Her face was drawn and her body thin. Meredith didn't have to look closely to see the bruise across her eye. There would be more visible on her arms if she moved the covers away.

"What did Daddy do to you last night?" she asked her.

"Your daddy didn't do anything, baby." Another muffled sob issued from her throat. She had never lied very well.

"Ma, you have to do something about him. You have to stop him from hitting you. Call the police. Leave him. For God's sake *do* something!"

"I can't leave him, baby. Just look how sick I am. Who'd take care of me? Nobody cares about me now. Never stay home. Always gone. Looks like somebody'd care how sick I am." She closed her eyes and drew her legs up closer to her chin, pulling the covers up with them. The blankets trembled and shook as she quivered, as if a cold draft had run through her body.

Meredith shivered watching her. "Momma, listen to me. I'm not going to be here forever to take care of things for you. I'm nearly twenty-one years old. I

29

have a business of my own. You have to start taking care of yourself. Go up to New Jersey and stay with Aunt Thelma. I have to get away from here." The silence in the room was so complete that the only sound Meredith heard was her own breathing. "Did you hear me, Momma? I'm going to leave. For good."

A picture flashed through her mind of her mother as a younger, healthier woman. She remembered when her home had seemed orderly and secure because her mother had made it that way. Then it had all changed when her father had started to drink heavily.

Meredith would not have continued to live at home if Jessie had been willing to leave her father, no matter how much her mother claimed to need her. When she was seventeen she had apprenticed herself to a sign painter in Lone Point and had become quite skillful. Now she found herself much in demand for freelance jobs painting names on boats and signs for businesses in nearby towns. It was good work and she enjoyed the traveling and meeting new people.

"Momma, did you hear me? I'm leaving here. I'm going to move in with Jessie."

The eyes of the woman in the bed snapped open. They were filled with fear and something else, something like a thinly veiled hatred. "You don't love your family any more, Meredith. You've become an ungrateful daughter. Always going off somewhere. You care more about your friends than you do your family."

"No, I don't, Momma. I love you all. It's just that I can't stay here. I can't let him make a slave out of me the way he has you! I won't! I have to have a life of my own. I have to —"

Her mother's eyes flashed hot with an energy that

30

Meredith had not expected. It startled her into silence.

"You think I don't know what you've been up to, don't you? You think you've been fooling me just because I'm sick. Well, I know, Meredith. I know. Your brothers tell me what people say. People gossip in a small town."

"Mother, what are you talking about?" Her blood had turned to ice.

"I know all about you and that Andrews girl." She half rose from the bed, then fell back. "It's a crime against nature, Meredith. God will punish you. God doesn't like for people to do bad things. Or think bad thoughts either. You see what he's done to me? I thought bad thoughts about your father and you see what God's done to me! He'll punish you, Meredith! The Lord will punish you for sure!"

Meredith reacted to the hysteria in her mother's voice by standing and drawing back against the door frame as if she had been struck. The sobs that issued from her mother's body cut through to the marrow of her bones. She felt hot and cold and clammy at once. Rising anger caused her to tremble visibly. "What I do is none of your business, Mother! You and Dad have made your own choices in your lives for good or ill. Now I'm going to make mine!"

A muffled weeping pursued her as she walked rapidly back to the kitchen. On the shelf above the sink were all the bottles. The Valium. The Xanax. She picked up the bottles one by one. They had become the enemy. Her mother's illness lived in her mother's own mind. The doctors had as much as said so. But still they gave her the pills. Those emotion-taming, cooling-out, tranquility-giving pills

31

that after a while didn't work any more except to sentence her mother to a zombie's life.

In the morning hours that followed, Meredith found herself looking at the familiar bits and pieces of her own life as she went from room to room cleaning and straightening. Several times she paused to look in on the woman in the bedroom. Was this woman really her mother? Could she really call this house her home?

Somehow she didn't think so. Her home was with Jessie and she was going to make that happen. She had waited long enough. Now it was time.

Chapter Three

1

Jessie thought she was dreaming. Or maybe she wasn't. The voices seemed real enough. But the trees were all wrong. There were pine trees with coconuts. Purple orchids clung gamely to oaks and elms. From the throat of an orchid, a voice she thought she knew whispered loudly. It was a voice that jarred her sensibilities like biting into a green persimmon.

"You work all your life and do the very best you can do," the flower-phantom voice hissed, "and they

33

all die and leave you anyway. Don't trust the bastards! You can't trust anybody! Life's a bitch."

She wanted to cry out in agreement. To tell the soulful voice she knew just how it felt. Always, always, bad news. Always the life of Job.

"He's dead, my love. D-E-A-D. Do you know what I mean? Dead, as in gone. Gone forever and ever, forever and ever." A cackle followed the message which rose from the center of a brown pine-coconut.

"I won't take any more of your fuck-ups!" another voice screamed. "You killed him when I told you not to! I ought to do the same to you!"

"Please, don't kill him," she tried to say, tried to say to the flower voice, but she was cemented to the bed, her vocal cords riveted together.

"Don't kill who?" she asked herself. "How would I know?" she said in reply. "Just don't kill him, please, or you'll die!"

"Go search the boat." Then silence.

Time went by while she watched the orchids grow and flower kaleidoscopic blossoms. But the time had no meaning and went on for an eternity.

"Maybe it's in the truck," the first voice said as if it came from far away, "in the truck, in the truck, in the truck." The echo was maddening.

"But we searched the truck yesterday . . . day . . . day."

The voices kept moving undulating, until they were just echoes, ping-ponging crazily inside her head. And then the flowers and the voices were gone.

Sometime later, reality asserted itself. Jessie heard a truck motor, idling smoothly. Then it stopped. She sat up straight on the bed.

Her clothes were heavy with sweat. She was sure

she had heard her father's voice. Had it been in the next room? In the yard? But her father was dead, wasn't he? Yes. Dead. As in gone. Forever. And ever.

The window seemed like obsidian as she rose and peered into the darkness. Her mind stretched to reconstruct the day. She had thrown herself across the bed exhausted after Owens had left, and had dropped off into an instantaneous deep sleep. Had she been dreaming? What had awakened her?

A truck. Someone or something was tapping softly on the front door. Visions of comic book horror stories she had read as a kid flashed through her sleep-dulled head. *Tales of the Undead.* What if it were her father leaning heavily against the door? What if his flesh had begun to rot and his clothes were hanging, torn and shredded? What if she opened the door and got the bejesus scared out of her?

"Jessie! Jessie? It's me!" a voice shouted.

"Yeah? Who's me?" she asked in a high-pitched tone. She hesitated, trying to give her brain a chance to blow the smoke out.

"It's Sheriff Todd, Jessie. Mel Todd. I brought your truck home. I need to talk to you. Can I come in?"

Jessie forced herself to the front door. The tangy smell of the tide marsh came in with the breeze.

Todd waited for her face to register recognition before he began. "I'd planned to bring the truck back tomorrow, but we had a call over this way so I just had the deputy follow me here. He can take me back to the office."

"Sure," Jessie said finally, stepping back out of the doorway. "Come on in the kitchen. I'll make you some coffee. I'm afraid I was asleep."

Had it been Todd and the deputy she heard?

"I don't know if you're up to this, but you asked me to let you know when we knew something else — about your father. We got the preliminary autopsy report late this afternoon," Todd told her, and settled his body into a kitchen chair. He was a sinewy man with pale brooding eyes, set deep in his head. His face was long, with a narrow nose that shadowed his pointed chin. When he smiled he seemed to change into another man, for he had laugh lines everywhere and his eyes twinkled and gave off warmth and charm. But he was not smiling now.

"I want to know," she said, after putting a heaping spoonful of Mountain Blend in his cup.

"Well . . ." he said, his voice trailing away, then coming back strong, "your father drowned. Lungs were full of salt water. That's what actually was the cause of death, according to the coroner."

Oh yeah, sure, she thought. My old man routinely fell off the dock. Fell out of his boat too. Crazy man. Thought he could walk on water. Thought he could fly too. Some days he was Jesus. Some days, Superman. Faster than a speeding bullet. Eyes fell out when he was flying.

Out loud she said, "Is that all they found?" She handed him his coffee mug and took a swallow from her own. "'Cause we both know that's not all that happened."

"Maybe you'd rather not hear this. Just say so if that's the case. But no, that's not all they found." Todd was worrying his coffee with a spoon even though he drank it black.

Jessie's red-rimmed eyes grew watery, and for a moment she looked as if she was about to weep. She

36

felt the hair on her arms stand up and the blood in her face drain down into her stomach. She sat down to keep from falling. In a voice that was laden with dread, she said, "I want to hear it."

"They found burn marks, like from a rope, on his ankles and his wrists. It hurts me to say this, Jessie, but it looks like he was tortured first. Like they were trying to get him to tell them something. Then they drowned him. And mutilated his body." He added the last in a whisper under his breath.

Jessie put her hands over her face and sat that way for a minute. Then she stood up slowly and stared out the window into the darkness as she tried to sort out her feelings and to understand what was happening to her world. Silence hung like a tent over them both.

When she could speak, she said loudly, "*Damn* who ever did this! I'll kill him!"

"Now Jessie," Todd said, "I don't think you want to do anything rash."

"I don't know what to think, Sheriff," she replied more quietly. "I know he had some enemies, but I always thought he was too good a person to get into any kind of *real* trouble. I guess I thought at first you'd find out there was some maniac on the loose who did it. I hoped something like that anyway."

Todd laid his hand across his eyes like a man who has seen too much evil in his days on earth. Then he looked up into her face. "I wish I could tell you I don't think he *was* in trouble, but it's for damned sure something got him killed. People around here sometimes get into fist fights, but they hardly ever go so far as to kill each other. Jessie, I'm asking you to stay out of it. Right now, we don't know what happened or what might happen next. I've already warned you that you might be in danger too. And I sure don't want to fish your body out of the bay one of these days."

Todd felt a little better when she said, "Yeah. I guess you're right." He just wished he was sure he could believe her.

2

By one o'clock in the morning a curtain of clouds had rolled in, smothering any light that might have come from the moon. In the distance lightning made stabbing motions at the horizon.

Jessie sat stiffly in the truck cab at the end of the lane that led to Meredith's house. She tried to think rationally, but her mind kept filling up with useless clutter. She needed to talk things over with Meredith.

Her eyes caught a glimpse of her own face in the truck's side mirror as the cooling engine began a hollow *ping ping ping* sound. She stared as if in a trance into the drawn face of the stranger who looked back at her. She wanted to be with Meredith. To have her come to live with her, but now . . .

A stroke of lightning split the sky almost over her head, and she flinched. The thunder that followed seemed to set her free and she reached for the door handle.

"You fucking coward. Tell her what you want," she said out loud, then started down the lane toward Meredith's house. A cold spatter of rain smacked her on the head and trickled down the side of her face.

Dime-size drops began to beat the ground like tiny tom-toms.

Jessie stopped for a moment about halfway to the house, still unsure. The rain came down harder, finding its way into the collar of her fatigue jacket and onto the back of her neck. The dusky dirt smell of the woods rose up in her nostrils as the rain began its soaking. She took an indecisive step back in the direction of the truck. Then she saw a light moving through the woods, swinging back and forth while doing an up-and-down dance step. Someone was running toward her carrying a flashlight.

She wiped a hand across her face, trying to clear away the steadily falling rain. She fought the panic and the urge to charge blindly back toward the truck.

Then, the familiar voice: "Wait, Jessie, wait! I'm coming. Wait for me! Jessie!" Meredith threw herself against Jessie and clutched her body with the strength of someone drowning.

As Jessie stepped backward to look at Meredith's face, a bolt of lightning illuminated the sky and she saw the blood. A thin trickle from her temple, pale with rain but blood nonetheless.

"Oh Jesus, Meredith, you're hurt. Who hurt you?"

"Nobody hurt me, Jess. I was freaking out, wanting to talk to you. I started across the woods. I was going to your house."

"I should have called you to let you know I was coming. I was wrong last night. I thought I could handle this alone — should do it alone — but I just can't be without you." Jessie pulled her close again, suddenly sure of what to do.

Meredith was gasping from her run across the woods and from panic. "I wasn't positive you were home . . . I tried to phone you, but nobody answered. I almost didn't go but I was so afraid something had happened to you. Then two men were watching . . . from the woods . . . they were watching your house!"

"Oh, Christ. Shh, now," Jess said, trying to calm her down. "It's okay now. It's all right. All right."

"They're still out there, Jessie," Meredith said in a scared voice. "They watched you leave in the truck. They were coming up from the boat when you came out of the house. Then they hid in the woods."

Sheriff Todd's warning of danger came to Jessie's mind. Her stomach did a flip-flop.

"I stayed where I was," Meredith went on, her words still labored. "I thought maybe they'd leave, but I was afraid to move . . . afraid they'd come after me if they saw me."

"Could you tell who they were?" Jessie asked her. "Was it Clarence Owens?"

"It was too dark to see. When I saw you leave, I ran this way. I hoped you'd come over here — to get me," Meredith added. "I guess I cut my face on the tree branches."

Jessie stared out into the darkness. The voices had been real, not a dream. The thought made her scalp tingle. "Listen, Meredith, I think this is probably a mistake, but if you still want to, if you're not afraid, I want you to move in with me."

Without hesitation, Meredith replied, "I'll get my things later, but shouldn't we call the cops about the men?"

"Let 'em have whatever they can find! As far as I know, there's nothing there worth having. Right now, I need to think. We're going to just ride around for a while. Come on."

3

Even while Jess and Meredith were talking, Griffin Rather was busy ransacking Jessie's house. Eddie D'Amato was sitting in one of the kitchen chairs staring at the light fixture and smoking a cheroot. D'Amato's bulbous belly hung down over his belt. His blue leisure suit threatened to split its seams.

"Bastard," he said to the light. "Damned stubborn bastard!" Something in his brain told him that Andy Andrews could have been made to talk. Should have been forced to tell them where he had hidden it before Rather killed him. A bad mistake, killing him before they got the truth out of him. A mistake they'd pay for dearly if the package didn't turn up soon.

Minutes later Rather stuck his curl-frizzled head through the kitchen door. "Not here, boss. Been through everything — drawers, cupboards, closets. Even checked up the chimney." A short, emaciated body followed the head into the kitchen.

"Son of a bitch," D'Amato swore under his breath. He impatiently ran his hand through his black slicked-down hair. "What in the name of sweet bleeding Jesus did he do with the damned stuff?" Rather asked. His voice sounded like Peter Lorre in a grade B movie. D'Amato had often wondered if he deliberately talked that way.

"What are we gonna do now, Eddie?" Rather whined. He had no real courage. Just the killer instincts of a cornered rat that made him strike, then ask questions later.

D'Amato looked into Rather's skinny, pimply face

41

with frustration and disgust. Hands trembling, he reached inside his coat and pulled out a silver flask. He took a long swig. "Fuck you, Griffin. I'm gonna tell the big man you snorted the friggin' stuff."

Rather's eyes grew huge and round. "Like hell, you are!" he sputtered. "Oh no, you're not gonna blame this one on me!" He put his hands over the crotch of his wear-slicked cords as if that would protect him.

"You snot-nose freak! You better, by God, try to think of something! This is all your damned fault anyway, you stupid weasel. You couldn't wait to kill him!" D'Amato seemed to jump straight up, knocking over the kitchen chair as he ascended. He had that paradoxical agility of certain heavy men. His eyes blazed as he grabbed the collar of Griffin's shirt and lifted him off his feet, shaking the smaller man like a terrier shakes a snake.

Rather looked helplessly up into D'Amato's burning eyes. He briefly considered kicking him hard in his middle before he choked out, "Put me down, Eddie, you bastard! The girl must have it. That's the only thing left. He must of given it to her."

"Then I think," D'Amato said evenly, setting the smaller man on his feet again with exaggerated gentleness, "that you better figure out what to do about it. And you better go after her *right now* before she gets any farther away!"

4

Meredith woke from an exhausted sleep about three o'clock in the morning. She lay still for a long while, her head pillowed on Jessie's right thigh. The windshield wipers smacked back and forth in rhythm with her sluggish heartbeat. She reasoned that they must be somewhere in Virginia by now. Jessie had told her only that she wanted to ride around for a while to think. Then she had headed across the Potomac River. Meredith smiled to herself in the darkness, thinking that Jessie's whole life revolved around rivers and bays. They seemed to give her peace.

"Where are we, Jessie?" she asked in a sleepy voice.

"On our way to paradise, sooner or later," Jessie answered.

"Paradise, Maryland," Meredith said with a tiny sigh. "I've never heard of that town."

Jessie rubbed her hand along Meredith's smooth cheek. "Yeah, Paradise, Maryland, love. Paradise is anywhere you and I can live happily ever after."

Meredith sat up, brushing her fine hair away from her face. She yawned softly and stretched. "I like it when you call me love. But Jessie, Paradise, Maryland! That is so corny! Jessie, you are so full of shit!"

Jessie reached playfully for her in the darkness and pulled her close. She ran her work-roughened hand back and forth over Meredith's hair and still damp jacket. "Aren't you cold?" she wanted to know. "I can turn on the heater."

"I don't know." She looked at Jessie. "I think I'm just happy thinking about living with you. I can't seem to feel much else."

"Yeah, me too. That's mostly what I've been thinking about."

"Jessie, where are we going, really?"

"We'll be heading back home soon. I've just been driving. We're just over the Virginia line, heading south on I-95."

Meredith played with the dial on the radio until a voice said she had Fort Wayne, Indiana. Madonna was instructing her papa not to preach. When she finished, Kenny Rogers came on arguing that they don't make 'em like they used to.

Jessie let the speedometer climb a little higher. They had the interstate to themselves. No need to loaf along.

Twenty minutes, and then thirty went by. Out in the blackness a blue and white specter of a sign flashed its message: REST AREA 2 MILES AHEAD.

Jessie broke the calm. "Want to stop?"

"Might as well. I could stand to move around a little bit. I was about to go back to sleep."

5

Griffin Rather slowed the Buick down for the first time when he reached the toll booth at the Potomac River Bridge. The girl couldn't be far ahead of him. A sixth sense told him that she had headed south, but once over the bridge he knew he couldn't be certain what route she might have taken.

"Been very busy tonight?" he asked the man in the toll booth. In the bright lights he could see the man's stooped body and wrinkled cheeks. Old turkey probably needs money to supplement his lousy retirement, he thought.

"Not much traffic on a night like this," the man

answered. "Little rain always keeps people off the highways. See more folks out in the snow than in the rain. Guess they like to look at the snow fall."

"Haven't seen a black Dodge pickup come this way, have you? Young girl driving?"

The man counted out change for a ten into Rather's outstretched hand. "What you want to know for?" He eyed Rather in a suspicious way, looking at him sideways.

"My niece," Rather answered. "Her momma . . . my sister . . . sent me after her. Ran away from home. Has a boyfriend stationed down at Langley Air Base in Hampton. We think she's probably headed down that way."

"Kids these days," the old man snorted. "Always running off to some place. Not like the old days. No sir."

Rather nodded in serious agreement. He folded a five dollar bill in half and handed it back to the man. "Be a big help to me if you could remember. I'm not absolutely sure she came this way."

Palming the fiver, the fellow told him, "I did see her. Tell you why I remember. She was a looker, but big for a girl. Had a pretty little blonde gal with her. Right? Camper shell on the pickup."

"That'd be her all right," Rather said, trying not to look surprised. It hadn't occurred to him that she might not be alone. "Guess she brought her girlfriend along."

"Well, I wish you luck, good buddy. She's not too far ahead of you. Don't let none of them Smokey Bears give you no green stamps," he chuckled, lapsing into a southern trucker's CB drawl.

45

"Negatory, good buddy," Rather drawled back. "I'll watch out for Smokey for sure."

He left the toll booth on the double, wondering who the girl might have with her. As soon as he was well over the bridge, he let the Buick have its head, not worrying about any Smokies that might be patrolling the highway. He had to catch her before she made any more turns. His life depended on it.

6

"Jessie, you keep looking in the mirror. You don't think anybody is following us, do you?" Meredith crawled out of the pickup in the parking lot of the Rest Area and stretched her limbs in an attempt to get her circulation going again.

"I haven't seen any car lights behind us since we crossed the Potomac. You never can tell though. I want to get back on the road as soon as possible. Seems safer in the car."

"Aren't you scared? You seem so calm and in control of things."

Jessie laughed deep in her throat. "Good thing you can't take a look at my insides." She recalled too clearly the blind panic she had felt seeing Meredith's flashlight swinging through the trees back in the woods. Now she was more exhausted than anything else.

She threw Meredith a long look of adoration. Meredith's hair was just shoulder-length, a glimmering perfect blonde-white in the lights of the rest area. Sleep had softened her features, giving her a soft-round cherubic look, a look so beautiful that it made Jessie hurt.

Jessie glanced around the parking lot and was glad to see that they weren't alone. A gray station wagon with North Carolina plates was parked two spaces up. Two kids were sleeping in the back seat. Up at the other end of the parking lot was a custom van with something painted on its side. In the dim light she could barely make out a rather silly-looking fire-breathing dragon painted with its head thrown back in menacing fashion toward the van's rear.

A young woman with a baby in her arms came out of the women's bathroom and started toward the station wagon. She nodded a friendly hello as she passed Jess and Meredith on the walkway.

The men's room door burst open with a bang as they approached the rest stop building. A young man with long curly hair and a cruddy-looking beard hustled out. They could see him clearly in the lighted area surrounding the building. He had dragon tattoos running up each arm, the dragons' heads turned back toward their tails. The van's owner, Jessie thought.

Jessie's heartbeat became jittery but settled down as he walked on by without so much as a glance. She looked back in time to see him pull a tightly rolled joint out of his back pocket. Good old Mary Jane. No danger from him. He had other things on his mind.

"Wash your face and you'll wake up a little," Jessie told Meredith as they entered the washroom. "I'll need you to talk to me so I can stay awake."

"Oh, I can keep you awake without talking," Meredith answered with a sly grin and wink.

Five minutes later they headed back down the

path toward the pickup. Neither of them felt like talking. Each had her own private thoughts.

The station wagon was gone. In its place was a dark late-model car. Jessie pulled her breath in sharply. She glanced in as she walked by the car. No one was inside. She glanced around for other vehicles, but saw only the van at the other end of the parking lot.

"Get in quickly," she said to Meredith.

"What's the mater?"

"I don't know. Just get in!"

A man stepped out from behind the truck just as Meredith's door came open. His right hand held a shotgun, the barrel resting across his other arm. It was pointing at Meredith's chest.

"Move around on this side of the truck if you don't want to see me blow a hole in your girlfriend," he said in Jessie's direction.

"Oh shit!" Meredith muttered.

"Take it easy," Jessie said. She moved slowly away from the driver's door and came around the front of the truck as he had ordered. Now the gun was pointing at both of them.

"Keep your arms down at your side and don't make any fucking quick moves," the man said in a high-pitched voice. He seemed wired.

"Listen, fella," Jessie said with faked courage. "I don't know what you're up to, but you're not going to get away with it. Somebody's going to drive in here any minute."

Rather laughed. There were black stains under the arms of his shirt. "Ain't nobody out here in the middle of the night, little lady. And that fellow back there in the van, he's blasted. I checked." But he

48

glanced quickly behind himself as if he were not so sure of what he was saying. "You just walk nice and easy around to the other side of my car and get in the back seat," he told them.

"Jessie?" Meredith said, not sure what she should do.

"Better do what the nice man says, Meredith. Move to the other side of his car."

"Fucking-A. You do that, lady. Best for you not to give this ol' double-barrelled poker no trouble," Rather said.

The two women moved slowly around in front of the hood. Jessie prayed that car lights would appear in the entrance to the parking lot. Her brain raced through all the TV plots she had ever seen where somebody outwitted the man with the gun, but nothing would come that fit the situation. Where were Cagney and Lacy when you needed them?

"What do you want with us?" Meredith asked him.

"Nothing much," Rather replied with a smirk. "Just a little matter of a quarter of a million bucks, give or take a thousand or two."

"We don't have that kind of money, man!" Jessie projected loudly out over the parking lot. "You're barking up the wrong tree!"

"Shut your mouth, bitch!" he almost screamed. "You know exactly what I'm talking about. Get in the goddamn car."

Meredith had already crawled in the back. For a crazy, fleeting second, Jessie almost grabbed for the gun. She tried to imagine the sting of buckshot passing through her. Then she remembered that he would probably shoot Meredith too.

49

The inside of the car smelled new except for the faint stench of cigar smoke and bourbon. Jessie felt the prickle of velour fabric on her arm as she climbed in.

"Now lean over the front seat," he said, "with both your arms hanging down." He opened the front door on the passenger's side.

Jessie watched him pull a ball of small nylon rope from his back pocket. Her mind raced back to the marks the sheriff had said were on her father's arms and legs. For a split second her vision flashed red and she felt her temples pounding.

"You son of a bitch!" she screamed at him as she suddenly pitched her body forward into the front seat and to the left so that most of her weight lay on the horn. The blare spewed out into the night like a New Orleans trumpet at a wake.

"Run, Meredith!" she yelled and then, "Run for your life!"

But instead of running, Meredith jumped out and furiously began pounding on the hood of the car like a crazy person. Griffin Rather froze in his tracks as if the noise had thrown him into suspended animation.

"Put that gun down!" Meredith screeched. "I said *put that gun down!*"

Jessie's body was wedged between the steering wheel and the front seat, facing Rather. Out of the periphery of her vision, she saw movement. Meredith was climbing over the hood of the car.

"Run, Meredith!"

Jessie watched in disbelief as Meredith got down

on her hands and knees on the car hood and spit full in the man's face.

"*You spit on me,*" Rather cried out and wiped at his face, letting the barrel of the shotgun drop. His left hand seized the top of the passenger's door in a death grip as if he were afraid the asphalt might open up next and swallow him.

A quick surge of adrenalin hit Jess full force. Without a thought, she grabbed at the door handle and pulled it toward her with all her might. The crunch of Rather's fingers could be heard for just a brief moment before he began to wail, adding harmony to the horn sound which seemed to have taken on a life of its own. She could see the blood pouring from each of his fingers down the inside of the padded door.

"Got you now," Jessie muttered to herself.

"My hand!" Rather shrieked. "My hand! My fucking hand! You broke my goddamned hand, you bitch." The shotgun dropped to the pavement with a clatter as he pulled on his arm with his right hand, trying desperately to free his fingers from the car door's vise grip.

At the sound of the falling gun, Meredith vaulted onto Rather's shoulders and began riding him piggyback, pulling back hard on his kinky hair. "Leave us alone!" she yelled at the top of her voice. "What do you think you're doing, you pile of shit!"

Jessie, still wedged in the front seat, stared, then found her voice: "*Get the gun!*"

Meredith scrambled to the ground out of sight.

Rather's eyes stood out in their sockets like a

cartoon character's as his body seemed to grow smaller.

Meredith was standing behind him, her hands wrapped tightly around the business end of the shotgun.

Jessie watched in wonder as Rather's body seemed to fly forward toward the hood of the car. She heard a series of soft *pop-pop* sounds as his finger joints dislocated from his finger bones. The bloody white fingertips still showed clearly inside the top of the car door holding him fast. Meredith had hit him full force with the gun as if she were teeing off with a golf club.

"Go!" Jessie yelled to Meredith. "Go to the truck!"

Meredith took one more swing at Rather's head then started running. "I'm out of here!" she squawked.

Jessie reached behind her and gave the door handle a solid yank. The door popped open immediately, spilling her backward onto the pavement. She heard, rather than felt, her head crack sharply. Red, white and blue fireworks lit up inside her brain.

Then Meredith was standing over her, pulling her across the parking lot by her jacket. The bouncing of her head on the blacktop sent another flash of agony through her.

"Don't worry, I got him! I got the bastard! I got him! I got him!" Meredith was parroting mindlessly as she dragged her toward the truck.

For a crazy instant, Jessie thought she might be paralyzed, then the second rush of adrenalin hit her. Her feet hit the pavement running. A voice was screaming, "Get in the truck! Get in the truck!" Finally she recognized it as her own.

The truck engine caught immediately, sending another blinding spear of pain through her head. Jessie hauled the truck wheels up over the curbing, then swung violently back into the parking lot. The tires squealed as she floored the accelerator. In a final glance back in the rearview mirror, in spite of the darkness, she thought she could still see Rather's hand held tightly by the door.

Chapter Four

1

Diablo's Island is in the Chesapeake Bay, fifteen miles off the western shore of Maryland and east of the mouth of the Potomac River. Tourists inquiring into the source of the island's name may be told that Captain John Smith attempted to explore it in the early sixteen hundreds and encountered a tribe of giant Indians so warlike and vicious that he ever after referred to them as "those devils of the Chesapeake." Other tales have the island being used as an occasional safe haven for that devilish terror of the Atlantic shipping lanes, Edward Teach. Old Blackbeard himself. Both of these are legends, pure and simple.

What is authentic, for there are records to prove it, is that no modern family or group of individuals has ever lived on the island for more than a few years at a time. Some residents of Maryland's eastern shore, who tend to be a bit more superstitious than their western shore brothers and sisters, claim the island is the earthly home of the Devil himself who refuses to share it with mortals. Most likely, it is the vicious summer mosquitoes who are reluctant to share it, and the unpredictable fall hurricanes that sweep up into the bay that have made it seem uninhabitable. Or perhaps living on an island where all supplies have to be delivered by boat, however romantic that may seem, turns out to be just too much trouble for most people. Whatever the reason, Diablo's Island has been abandoned, and nearly forgotten, throughout most of the twentieth century.

In the early 1980s, the state of Maryland began to auction off property on which taxes had not been paid for many years. Archibald Coxson acquired the island for a small sum. The mansion he built on it was impressive, to say the least. It took him almost a year to have the redwood and teak and glass and brass brought over by boat from Baltimore. When it was finished, the inside of the large house was remarkably beautiful. Had he operated a ferry and opened the house to the public as a tourist attraction, he might have made a comfortable living off the price of admission, but, from the beginning, he had had other plans.

2

Just before the sun edged up over the horizon, Coxson was on his way to the two hundred foot pier that faced directly south on Diablo's Island. His motorized wheelchair moved swiftly along the wooden ramp that ran down the gentle slope from the house to the pier. He had had ramps built all over the island so that there was not one point, no matter how distant, that he could not reach on his own and unassisted. Independence is the mark of the man, he liked to say.

"Morning, Mr. Coxson," a voice said in the waning darkness. "Want me to turn on the floodlights so you can see better, sir?" A man stood at the base of the pier, blocking the entrance with his well-conditioned body. At his feet lay an oversized, solid white German shepherd. The dog had barely lifted his ears at the sound of the familiar wheelchair.

"No need for that, Mr. McSwain. Moonlight will be enough if the clouds hold back a little longer. Just open the gate for me."

McSwain switched the rifle from his right hand to his left and reached for the chain link gate that separated the pier from the island. It was part of a continuous fence that ran, eight feet high, around the circumference of the five-mile island. At each quarter-mile point along the fence, another guard and German shepherd, all white, men and dogs, were posted. The guards and the dogs were trained to kill any stranger who approached the island unannounced.

"Red cast in the eastern sky," McSwain told Coxson. "Not going to be much of a day for good weather." He opened the gate and stepped wide to allow the wheelchair to pass easily. The dog moved smartly behind McSwain without being spoken to.

"You never know about the weather, Mr. McSwain. God's work and you never can tell about God! God moves in mysterious ways, you know?"

"As you say, Mr. Coxson," McSwain replied in his best military fashion. "Sir, Mr. D'Amato is waiting in his boat at the end of the pier. I asked him to remain there until you came."

"Too bad it didn't sink while he waited," Coxson said out loud but to himself. "Son of a bitch doesn't know his ass from a hole in the ground." He put his finger on the button marked FORWARD and the wheelchair moved smoothly ahead. The low whirring of the well-oiled motor echoed back to him off the water.

D'Amato's boat was a twenty-one foot Sea Ox with open bow and a center console. He sat in the captain's chair behind the wheel staring moodily out over the bay. Coxson was nearly at the end of the pier before D'Amato heard him approaching. Startled, D'Amato jumped too quickly to his feet. His belt buckle caught neatly under the steering wheel, almost jerking his pants down as he stood up. "Shit," D'Amato grumbled as he pulled his pants back up to the proper location under his stomach. His nerves were strained to the hilt.

"And God bless you, too, Mr. D'Amato," Coxson shot back. "Red sky this morning. Sailor take warning. Ever heard that one, Mr. D'Amato? Rain, likely."

"Yes, sir. Considerable rain when I left the mainland. Probably hit here before too long."

Coxson cleared his throat impatiently. "Guess

57

we'd better get on with our business quickly then."
He sat back in the wheelchair and folded his hands
in his lap, fingers intertwined.

"Right, sir, our business," D'Amato began, with a
nervous twitch in his voice. He chewed energetically
on the stump of his burned-out cigar. "Sir, our
business can't be completed right now. That's what I
came out here to talk to you about. You see, sir,
well, there's a problem."

Coxson raised his hands to his face, then made a
steeple toward the sky with his fingers. "Please, dear
God, for Mr. D'Amato's sake, don't let this be a
serious problem," he said toward the heavens.

D'Amato felt an involuntary shudder course
through his body. "You have to understand, sir, that
sometimes things just happen. Things are not always
under direct control. You're an intelligent man. You
know that."

Coxson folded his strong muscled hands in his lap.
As with most paraplegics, his healthy upper body had
developed in strength as his lower body wasted. "I
don't have to understand anything, D'Amato. Just
start from the beginning and don't waste my time
making ass-kissing excuses."

"Well, sir, you see, one of the watermen we
recruited has been killed. He agreed to take a
shipment, then the shipment disappeared. That is, he
didn't have it when we went to pick it up. He said
he was going to turn it, and us, over to the
authorities. Griffin and I stopped him from doing
that, sir, but he wouldn't say where the shipment
was." D'Amato was sweating profusely in the cool
morning air.

"And is it safe to assume, Mr. D'Amato, that you

58

used one of your famous heavy-handed methods to keep him from going to the law?"

"We killed him, sir. That is, Griffin Rather killed him. But the man had to be killed eventually, you can see that." D'Amato was breathing hard, his words coming out in little panting breaths.

"I can see, Mr. D'Amato, that you really are the brainless idiot I always thought you were!" Coxson exploded. "And I can see that you've lost a shipment worth a great deal of money, and that you've attracted attention I certainly don't need!"

"Well, no sir, we haven't lost the shipment." His voice trailed off to a whisper. "At least we haven't lost it completely."

Coxson raised his cold blue eyes to the sky. "Forgive me my sins, Lord, not the least of which is employing this stupid asshole standing before me." His gaze came back to D'Amato. He didn't like him. D'Amato was an excuse maker, and if there was one thing he couldn't abide, it was anyone who made excuses for his own stupidity.

"Sir," D'Amato pleaded, "it's not as bad as it sounds. His daughter has it. Or at least we're pretty sure she does. If she doesn't have it, she knows where it is."

"You stupid prick! If his daughter has it, why didn't you get it from her?"

"We are, sir. Getting it, I mean. Griffin has gone after her." And he added weakly, "Rather will get the cocaine."

"You idiotic pig. She can have the cocaine for all I care. But what if *she* tells what she knows about our little importing business?" Coxson bellowed. "Come here, McSwain. Now!"

McSwain appeared on the double, dog at his side.

"Take this idiot up to my office. Hold him there and don't let him move a muscle until I tell you otherwise."

"Yes, sir. Right away."

D'Amato opened his mouth to protest but only air came out. There was a brief instant in which he heard the first birds proclaim the rising of the sun, just before McSwain brought his billy club down across his skull and made the birds' singing come from inside his head.

3

The communications room was in the basement of Coxson's house. It was crammed full of electronic machinery, all state of the art. Twenty-five television monitors displayed pictures of strategic locations on the island. Coxson sat looking at the computer with which he kept track of his extensive business activities. The computer kept an accurate, moment-by-moment record of the location of each of his shipments, each of his boats and each of his employees. Information scrolled by on the screen. Five minutes later he had what he wanted. He reached for the intercom.

"Good morning, Miss Beck," he said.

"And to you, Mr. Coxson. Mr. Mendez is calling from Mexico City. He's holding on three."

"Tell him I'll call him later. Miss Beck, I'd like you to contact Mr. Anamus. Call him in Atlantic City. I want him in my office as soon as possible."

"He's not going to like it, sir. He's just started setting up the New Jersey operation.

"Miss Beck," he said with exaggerated patience. "I do recognize your very, how shall I say, personal concern for Mr. Anamus. But, Miss Beck, have you ever heard the old saying that one should keep away from bad company?"

A muffled giggle came back over the intercom. "Very good, sir. I'll contact him."

Coxson grunted. His eyes went back to the computerized file on the screen.

Nee: Walter Anamus, Richfield, New Jersey, November 20, 1958. Aka: Animal. Psychological Evaluation: Narcissistic personality with psychopathic dimensions. Extremely self-centered and self-confident in appearance. Thought processes dominated by paranoid content, bordering on psychotic delusions of both persecution and grandeur. Preoccupied with power and control of others. Capable of extreme violence, especially in the face of ego-threatening events. Handle with extreme care and consider dangerous at all times.

Coxson leaned forward on his elbow, his eyes staring blankly at the screen. He could almost see the man behind the words printed there. He felt the tiny hairs on his arms stand on end. Walter Anamus frightened him, and he wasn't easily frightened. So he had tried to use him sparingly. Only in emergencies. Like this one. Anamus was too good to waste. He knew how to get things done and Coxson couldn't

61

afford to have the Chesapeake Project blow up on him.

He reached for the intercom switch again. "I want all the computer files on the Chesapeake Project, Miss Beck. And call McSwain, up in my office. Tell him to take D'Amato and lock him up in the security area. I'll deal with him later. Oh, and call Mendez back and tell him to route his shipment through Vazquez in New York. Tell him, for right now, hold all shipments to the Chesapeake."

"Very good, Mr. Coxson." She paused. "Is something wrong, sir?"

"Nothing that you need to know about, Miss Beck," Coxson scolded. "Didn't anyone ever tell you, Miss Beck, that a little knowledge is a dangerous thing?"

Coxson loaded the disks he needed into the computer and began looking through the personnel files, locating D'Amato's first and then Rather's. How many people did he have working on the Chesapeake Project? One, two dozen? He had hired most of them himself in the beginning, but lately, with the development of new projects, he had left the hiring of new people, Rather and D'Amato for example, to others. A mistake. He hoped not an irreversible one. No time to slip up now.

His eyes drifted toward the TV monitors across the room. Number 3 was showing what looked like a war movie. Men in black fatigue uniforms were shooting at other men in white uniforms. Monitor 7 was scanning a parade ground. Troops stood at attention in black Nazi-style uniforms while they were being reviewed by officers in solid white. A moving and impressive sight, Coxson thought. He watched the monitors with pride for some time before turning back to the computer. He scanned information as it flashed across the amber screen.

He stopped as his eyes fell on an entry dated January 15, 1984. He read quickly:

Now that I have found an ideal location for my headquarters (and at a very good price I might add) it will be necessary to begin the fundraising. The Chesapeake Bay seems to be an ideal place to begin. There are tens of thousands of watermen going in and out of various ports each day. This will work out quite well, I believe. Eventually . . .

Then another entry dated April 16, 1984:

The fundraising has finally begun. Connections have been established in Mexico, Cuba, Puerto Rico, and Colombia. Others will follow. There are thirty-five watermen at present who have agreed (with some persuasion, of course) to pick up deliveries on their boats and take them ashore. Six wholesale seafood establishments in Maryland and Virginia have been purchased to receive and distribute . . .

And September 5, 1985:

The first men have arrived on the island for guerrilla warfare training. There are fifty in this first group, mostly misfits and malcontents to be sure, but they will serve my purpose. They will be trained by the finest noncoms and

officers that the United States has to offer.
The U.S. military should pay their men
better . . .

Coxson sighed. Overall things had gone very well.
Recruiting soldiers had been the least of his problems.
There seemed to be an endless supply of greedy and
unpatriotic young men who were more than willing to
become mercenaries in any man's army. True, two or
three had decided to take the money and run after
they had completed their combat training. But not
since early in 1986, when one was shot and killed on
the New Jersey Turnpike by an unidentified sniper.
Another committed suicide it seemed, but in a most
strange manner. The paper had said he had
swallowed an entire bottle of lye. Good examples were
a must in any organization. He had dealt with the
third one himself. There hadn't been a single deserter
since that unfortunate chap's head had sat on a post,
in the style of Blackbeard himself, staring blankly
over the parade grounds for a few days.
      Coxson sat back in his wheelchair and looked
thoughtfully across the room at the two pictures
hanging on the wall. Franklin Roosevelt on the right.
Then off to the left, Ralph Harrington, President of
the United States. "Gentlemen," he told them with
an exaggerated salute, "you have to take the sour
with the sweet."

4

It was eleven fifteen when he buzzed Miss Beck

64

on the intercom from his office. "Will you find Micky Bates and have him come in here?"

"He's been here, waiting for your call, since Mr. D'Amato was taken to security, sir. Shall I send him in?"

He wished he had more men like Bates. Always a step ahead of everybody else. Always ready to do what needed to be done.

"I want you to take charge of D'Amato, Micky."

"My pleasure, sir." Bates was fair and blond. Not tall. Not short. Just solid looking. He squared his already straight shoulders in the white officer's uniform that fit him like a second skin. He always looked as tailored and well-groomed as a soldier about to receive a medal.

"It has been some time now since we have had to discipline any of our men and I would like it to be a longer time before we have to do it again. Therefore, I want you to arrange something quite exotic for our Italian friend."

"You can count on me to do my best, sir."

"Yes, I am well aware of that," Coxson said, nodding approval. "I will let you decide the best way to deal with him. But, Micky, whatever you do, I want it done in the Chesapeake Bay near where he was stationed. Somewhere near Pliney Point, Maryland. And I want everybody in that area to be aware of what happens to him. Understand?"

"Understood. Should it look like an accident, sir?"

"No accident this time. I want it to look like exactly what it is. An execution. I want everyone who's involved in the Chesapeake Project to get the message that you don't fuck around when you work for Archibald Coxson. You have my permission to do whatever you wish, as long as that message is obvious."

Something in the young man's eyes looked almost like gratitude. Micky Bates loved nothing better than killing. He had not been born with a lust for blood-letting. No, it was an acquired taste which had come to him with the compliments of the U.S. Marines who had given him the training that enabled him to do it well, and the opportunity to find out what a wonderfully delightful feeling it brought. After his discharge, he had sought out the patriarch of the most powerful Mafia family in Chicago and offered his services as a hit man. It had been a comfortable arrangement for them both until two years before, when it had become necessary for him to murder a government agent. Then things had gotten sticky. Too sticky for him to stay in Chicago.

Don Carmona had told him in his Sicilian accent, "It is for the good of the *fratellanza* that you must leave us for a while, my son. The FBI will be crawling all over Chicago, trying to find you. They do not take lightly the killing of one of their own. But do not worry," he had said, smiling. "I have found a place for you to work where you will be happy and safe. And the family will be protected as well. There is a crippled man, a crazy man really, running drugs from the Chesapeake. You will go there, volunteer your services, and watch him. Report to me any changes. He will not do the *fratellanza* any real harm I think, and for now we will leave him alone. Perhaps one day, he may be of some use to us. We shall see."

The Don had sent him off to Diablo's Island with a father's blessing.

"Will that be all, sir?" Bates now said to Coxson.

Coxson hesitated and then said, "You're a fine young man, Micky. I'm lucky to have you working for me."

"Thank you, sir."

Coxson added as an afterthought, "How old are you?"

"Twenty-five, sir."

"A fine young man. I wish I could have had a son like you."

5

When the door had closed softly behind Bates, Coxson reached again for the intercom switch. "Has Animal arrived yet, Miss Beck?"

"His ETA is two o'clock."

"Send him in as soon as he arrives."

"I have a call holding for you, sir. It's Mr. Rather, calling from Maryland."

"All right, my dear. Put him through."

Coxson stared at the phone for a full two minutes before he picked it up. It would be good to let Rather sweat a little bit.

"Have you found the daughter, Rather?" He spoke into the phone abruptly, not telling him he had talked to D'Amato.

"How did you know . . ." Rather started in surprise, but recovered quickly. "Not yet, sir, but I have followed her."

"Then you know where she is?"

Rather's voice cracked when he replied, "No, sir, not exactly."

Coxson raised his eyes toward the ceiling. "God help you if you've lost her!"

"She took a girlfriend with her, sir. They . . . they got away from me. But sir," he continued in a pleading voice, "I know approximately where they are. I'll take care of it."

Coxson's voice exploded into the phone. "You listen to me, you motherfucking fool. If you can't handle two *little girls*, you've got no business working for me. Do you know what will happen if the police find out how we're getting our shipments in and out of —" Coxson closed his eyes and sighed. His pulse was throbbing in his temples. He breathed deeply, trying to relax. No need to risk a stroke on this piece of horse manure.

After a moment, he continued calmly, "I want you to stay wherever you are. You can tell Miss Beck where that is when I hang up. This afternoon I am sending Walter Anamus over to help you. And, Mr. Rather, you had better spend the time between now and then on your knees, praying to God that the girl does not know what her father was up to and tell the police."

Coxson hung up. He sat with his eyes cast down for a few minutes, massaging his withered legs. Sometimes they seemed to ache, even though they had long ago lost the capacity for any kind of pain. His eyes drifted back to the portrait of Ralph Harrington.

How many times had he replayed the scene? Harrington had returned to Viet Nam from Washington with the message that the war was moving too slowly; that the Marines were behaving timidly, letting the Army carry the burden of combat.

They were to immediately begin attacking main force units of the Viet Cong.

Two weeks later, in July of 1966, Harrington had ordered Coxson's unit up against overwhelming odds outside Da Nang. Harrington knew it was a stupid, meaningless mission, and Coxson knew Harrington was not concerned with the unavoidable devastation that was certain to occur. Coxson pleaded with him to combine his unit with one or two more, but Harrington had only laughed, saying that he could not afford to have Washington believe him a coward. The young Coxson was not the kind of Marine who could wage war against a superior with whom he disagreed, so he took himself and his men to the battlefield, while Harrington stayed safely in Saigon. If it weren't for Harrington, he *could* have had a son like Micky Bates. Someday Harrington would pay for creating those withered legs — and the limp penis between them. Goddamned if he wouldn't. Archibald Coxson had dedicated his life to it.

The buzz of the intercom interrupted his ruminations. "Mr. Anamus is here," Miss Beck said excitedly.

6

When the door opened, Walter Anamus towered on the threshold. He had to stoop slightly to clear the seven-foot doorway of the office. He was not a handsome man in the Hollywood sense. Not pretty. No Greek profile. He had the look of a man whose life had written itself all over his face. Miss Beck had once replied, when Coxson had chided her over her

69

attraction to Anamus, that he was the only man she had ever met whose appeal was his ugliness, rather than his good looks. To Coxson, he had the look of a punched-out boxer — like Sly Stallone with a thyroid problem. But his looks were not what Coxson responded to.

There was something about Anamus that made Coxson suspect that the air surrounding the large body actually vibrated, as if there were some kind of aura that might be visible with the right kind of glasses or if caught on the proper film. Coxson avoided touching him for fear that he would feel a shock or a force-field that would defy explanation and would make him more afraid of Anamus than he already was. And he was afraid. Anamus was the only person he ever met who completely terrified him. Coxson had long since resolved to keep him on his own payroll to be sure he never worked against him for someone else.

"You're early, Walter." Coxson never called him by his nickname to his face.

Animal flashed a large, toothy smile. "I knew that you wouldn't call me back from New Jersey unless there was some crisis. You wouldn't now, would you?" There was something almost sinister in his tone. "So I came as quickly as I could."

"Sit down, Walter." Then he added, "Please."

Anamus folded himself into the chair in front of Coxson's desk. He was wearing cut-off faded jeans and a skin-tight yellow pullover. The contours of his chest muscles looked like the kind of armor worn by Roman soldiers in the movies. He began to roll the dense black hair that covered his thighs

70

absentmindedly between his thumb and forefinger. His dark eyes bored straight ahead into Coxson's.

"How was Atlantic City?" Coxson asked, trying to sound pleasantly interested. Whenever he talked to Anamus he had an almost irresistible urge to sit on his hands and keep them from fidgeting.

"Not bad," the Animal said in a flat voice.

"Crowded this time of year?"

"You might say that." His habit of never volunteering information irritated Coxson.

Coxson waited for a few awkward moments, then cleared his throat loudly. "There's something I need you to do."

"I like to feel needed," Animal said curtly.

"It'll take a while to explain."

"My time is your time. Obviously. So tell me."

So Coxson told him. About Rather and the *girls*, as he called them. About the missing shipment. About how he was to leave immediately to be sure the Andrews girl was captured and brought to the island. What he didn't tell Anamus was how scared shitless he was that she would spill the beans about his cocaine importation business before she was caught.

When Animal left, some thirty minutes later, Coxson relaxed. A little. He closed his eyes and let his thoughts wander around inside his head until they came to rest on Ralph Harrington again. He could see it all in his mind's eye. Hundreds of highly trained men, all dressed in black, flooding the White House lawn. How will you feel, *Mr. President,* when you see troops, my troops, surrounding your precious White House?

Chapter Five

1

Jessie lay watching the rays of the late morning sun shoot yellow darts through the cracks between the slats of the Venetian blinds in her own bedroom.

Her head throbbed slightly as she tried to make herself more comfortable on the pillow. Her gaze shifted to the sleeping figure of Meredith. She frowned. *Meredith, my love, what have I gotten you into?*

As if Jessie's thoughts had somehow pierced

through the light haze of her morning sleep, Meredith opened her eyes and looked at her lovingly. She stretched her long naked limbs in sensuous feline fashion. "How can you possibly look so worried when here we are, alone behind a locked door? God! I was tired of making love in the woods or in your old Pontiac!" she said in a thick morning voice. She ran her finger lovingly along the deep cleft of Jessie's chin.

Jessie turned over in her direction, draping her sun-browned arm around Meredith's waist. She smiled broadly, flashing her deep dimples. "You don't worry about very much, do you, kid? That was some kind of stunt you pulled last night. Weren't you afraid when you spit in that guy's face? He could have killed you!"

"Don't call me *kid!* And no, I don't worry much. I used to, you know. For years and years I worried about my father's drinking and fighting, and I worried about my mother's illnesses. I worried about when I was going to get to live with you. And you know what? Nothing changed. It all stayed the same. So I quit. Worrying, I mean. It never helped me get one single solitary thing I ever wanted."

"You make it sound so simple. Wish it was that easy for me," Jessie said softly. "Meredith, you *must* appreciate the danger we're in. They're likely to kill us both if they decide to. For all we know, that frizzy-headed fellow will be back here any minute."

"Jessie, we have to find out what this is all about."

"I already *know* what it's about, Meredith. Dad got mixed up in something that was way over his head and got himself killed for it."

"That's what *happened*, sure, but you don't have any idea *why* it happened, Jessie. That's what we've got to know."

"Meredith, you never have known when to keep your nose out of things. The police are working on this. Just let it alone. Sheriff Todd told me in no uncertain terms to stay out of it and that's what I'm planning to do." Jessie's hands went to Meredith's shoulders to pull her to her, but Meredith resisted and sat up straight in the bed.

"Some rompin' stompin' dyke, you are! You liked to act tough in that bar in Baltimore, didn't you? Big hairy deal, wearing those white crabbing boots! Underneath it all you're just a chickenshit! All show and no action!"

A brooding look fell on Jessie's face and she sat up. "And just what is it you'd like me to do? Get my head blown off? That's exactly what could've happened to you last night, you know. It still could happen if that guy comes back here looking again."

"Listen," Meredith said, suddenly enthusiastic, "I've been lying here thinking half the night. Or what was left of it after we got back. That fella who came after us thought we had something worth a lot of money. I'll bet my ass it's drugs. Why don't we just pretend we have it, then we'll find out . . ."

"Meredith, Meredith, give me a break! This isn't some movie on TV! This is real life! And what in the world would my father be doing with drugs? He wouldn't even drink a bottle of beer! I don't believe you!"

Meredith got up abruptly, went to the window and pulled up the blind. She stared out the window as she spoke. "Jessie, I've always let you have everything your own way. You didn't want to leave your father and I didn't try to force you into it. And this time you can do what you want, too. If you don't want to try to find out who killed your father, you don't have to. But I'm going to try everything I can think of. And do you know why? Because until this is all settled I don't stand a chance of having one hundred percent of you and that's what I want. And," she added emphatically, "you're in danger and I can't stand that."

Jessie moved to stand behind her. "You're tired," she said, kissing her lightly on the back of her neck. "Come back to bed and get some rest. You'll feel different later."

Meredith turned toward her and snuggled her own body into Jessie's. "If I could only get you to understand how I feel about you. What I would risk, just to be with you all the time."

"Maybe you oughta tell me again how you *do* feel," Jessie said softly, as she cupped Meredith's breast with her hand. "You're the only really good thing that's ever happened to me."

Meredith looked up at her for a long moment, trying hard to find the right words. "I feel . . . I feel like I never want you to have to worry again. Like I never want you to be tired or lonely. Like I always want to be right here, by your side, loving you as strong as I can, no matter what bad things may happen. I want to keep *you* safe. I'll do anything I have to. You're the most important thing in my world, Jess."

Jessie reached for her again and pulled her close as she led her back toward the bed.

When they lay face to face, their breasts touching

75

lightly, Meredith whispered, "Jessie, do you remember once, when we were in Miss Barlow's class, we had to learn that poem about time?"

Jessie paid no heed to Meredith's words. Instead, she traced the edge of her ear with her fingertip, then leaned toward her to gently bite her neck.

Meredith went on single-mindedly, "I can't remember who wrote it but it went something like, 'Hold fast the time. Guard it and watch over it, every hour, every minute. Unregarded it slips away.' I bet you don't remember it, but that's how I feel about our life. I want to live every minute of it to its fullest."

"I remember this lovely body of yours," Jessie murmured in her ear as she continued to shower tiny kisses on her neck and down her shoulder.

Meredith pulled back a few inches, then laughed. "God, I'll never make a romantic out of you!"

With that, she rolled her body so that it lay the full length of Jessie's. Passionately, Meredith kissed her, sucking playfully, then urgently, on her tongue. After interminable minutes, she eased the pressure and lifted her mouth slightly, letting it linger there, motionless, but maintaining light contact. Her breath was labored and sweetly hot.

Jessie felt her body burning, as from the sun's heat. Then she increased the pressure on Meredith's lips and tried to give her all the feelings she held inside.

Meredith moaned slightly and broke away. "I love you so much," she murmured. "Don't you know how much it would hurt me to be away from you?"

"Meredith," Jessie began, but Meredith kissed her fiercely, possessively, as she thrust her body tight against her.

Hungrily, Jessie returned the kiss and slipped her fingers between their bodies, finding delicious wetness as Meredith began to press rhythmically, almost reflexively, against her.

"Is this romantic enough for you?" Jessie whispered in her ear. Then she moved her mouth slowly, sensuously, down the softness of Meredith's body until she reached her inner thighs.

Meredith moaned as Jessie's tongue worked the wanting into burning passion. "Talk to me, Jessie, say all the things I want to hear," she pleaded. "Tell me you love me, please. But don't stop. Oh, God, Jessie, don't stop!"

Jessie couldn't bring herself to tell her that she loved her more than her own life, but she made love to her with a desperation born of fear as well as love. And she didn't tell her of the self-doubt that lay at the threshold, threatening to eclipse her joy as Meredith's pleasure burst out at the end, in slight asynchrony with her own sharp orgasm.

2

Jessie came out of a troubled sleep to the sound of her gold-plated Timex, its tiny alarm buzzing loudly in the noontime bedroom heat.

"Meredith, get up. We've got to get the rest of your things and let your folks know where you are."

"I don't want them to know where I am and I don't intend to tell them." Meredith rubbed her eyes and made a grumpy face. "I didn't mean to go to sleep on you."

Jessie wiped a hand across her face. In spite of her restless sleep, she felt refreshed. She recognized her mellow feeling as the residue of their lovemaking. There was a tranquility about Meredith that Jessie pondered, until it occurred to her that it too might be the aftermath of sexual release.

"Jessie, just before I went to sleep I had an idea," Meredith said. Suddenly she sat straight up, full of energy.

"Well, my darlin', I guess we can use all the ideas we can get right now. I sure don't have very many." She looked at her, inquiring.

"I was thinking — don't get mad now, okay? I was thinking what it would be like if you were a man."

"Far out," Jessie said without enthusiasm. "Think I should have a sex change?"

"No, silly, I don't mean *physically* like a man. I happen to like you very much as a woman." She gave a sexy laugh as she reached out to touch Jessie's downy thigh. "I was just thinking that they, whoever *they* may be, are going to be looking for a woman. So maybe we could make you look like a man. If you had short hair, you could probably pass."

"Maybe," she said sharply, "but I don't think anybody around here would buy it. Forget that."

Meredith watched closely as Jessie got up and pulled on her jeans. There was a barely perceptible stiffening in her shoulders that warned Meredith that this was a touchy subject. She wished for a moment

78

she hadn't brought it up, but now that she had, she felt compelled to pursue it.

"Jessie, I don't mean that you look like a man. It's just that, well —" She fumbled for the right words. "Of the two of us, you look more like a man than I do."

Jessie laughed bitterly. "You don't say, José."

Meredith swung her feet to the floor and moved in behind her. Her voice was filled with unexpected power. "Jessie, look at me," she commanded. "All we'd need to do is disguise you as a man and move away from Pliney Point. Not too far. Even another town in this county. Maybe to Quinn's Inlet. I can paint signs anywhere if we need the money, just like you can crab anywhere. I can even crab with you. You know I've worked with my father when any of the boys were sick. Quinn's Inlet is the biggest town in the county. Do you know anybody over there?"

"No, Meredith, I don't, but I can't see how that's going to help us. I don't want to hide out for the rest of my life. And I don't want to be a man! People have always said to me, 'Don't walk like a man, Jessie. Don't talk like a man, Jessie. Don't sit that way. Don't stand like that.' And though they've never said it out loud, 'For godsake, Jessie, don't love a woman.' Men! Who needs 'em?"

Meredith gazed at her, startled. "Jessica Andrews, why are you being so damned difficult? You and I are in one hell of a mess right now. And I plan to live a long, long time so I can love you a long, long time. Now if you don't like any of my ideas, what are we going to do?" Meredith turned her around to look at her face.

They looked directly into each other's eyes for a

79

moment before Jessie burst out laughing. "We'll cut my hair first. Then we'll take that ever-loving pickup truck and have it painted bright red. We'll move over to Quinn's Inlet if that's what you want and then maybe, just maybe, I'll buy me a .30-.30 shotgun and a gun rack so I can ride around looking like some redneck good ol' boy! How does that grab you?"

"Just like this!" Meredith said. She threw her arms around Jessie's neck and hugged her with all her strength.

3

While Jessie's long chestnut hair was falling to the bathroom floor, Animal was crawling out of Coxson's private helicopter and into Griffin Rather's dark blue Buick. Their rendezvous had been set for a deserted logging camp five miles north of Pliney Point and seven miles east of Quinn's Inlet.

"I've heard a lot about you. People call you Animal. You don't mind if I call you that, do you?" Rather said as Anamus folded his large frame into the front seat of the car. He appeared not to notice the several bruises on Rather's face or his bandaged hand.

"Let's find someplace where we can get something to eat," Animal said, as if Rather had not spoken. "I've been flying all over hell and back since this morning and I'm starving."

"I was kinda hoping you might drive," Rather said.

Animal grunted loudly. "Only shitheads drive

80

cars," he said. "Never found any good reason to learn how when there's always somebody to do it for you."

Rather drove carefully, protecting his swollen fingers. "You from around here?"

Animal looked out the window and said nothing.

"Me, I grew up in Baltimore," Rather prattled nervously. He was trying to be cool. Animal's sheer size had him spooked. "The pride of Maryland. Lots of ways to boogie in that great city. Ever been there?"

The only response was a shrug from Animal.

"I always liked being a city dude. Learned a lot in the city. Street smart, you know?"

"Mister," Animal rumbled, "I don't give a damn about you or where you come from. Just pull into the first place you see that has food and try real hard to keep your mouth shut."

Fifteen minutes later they found a place where pink neon lights spelled out the unassuming name THE CAFE.

"Just look at this shit town," Rather cracked as he climbed out of the car. "Guess the rest of the two-bit joints are known as The Grocery Store and The Filling Station. What do you think, Animal?"

Animal's eyes took in everything at once. One filling station, a barber shop with an old-fashioned red, white and blue pole, a family-owned food store and a few worn-out houses. Rather had a point. Quinn's Inlet would hardly qualify as a tourist attraction, but this would make things a lot easier. Two unknown females would be likely to attract a lot of attention if they were here.

Rather chattered on about nothing as they went

into the diner and sat down in an empty booth. His good hand twisted pieces of his frizzy hair nervously as he talked. Animal motioned for the waitress.

"What you boys having?" she asked, rolling her hips in Animal's direction. "Blue plate special is liver and onions, two vegetables, rolls and your drink. How's that sound?"

Animal gave her a suggestive up-and-down look. She had the look of an aging Miss Apple Blossom. "You run this place, honey?"

"Yeah, sugar, I do. What you want to know for?"

"Just wondered. You like music?"

"Good as the next one, I guess," she answered, flashing a full Ipana smile at him. Her eyes moved appreciatively to his muscled chest.

"How about bringing us a couple of cold beers and filling up that old music machine over there with about five dollars worth of quarters? Keep the rest for yourself." He laid a twenty on the table and gave her a broad wink.

"You bet I will, sweet thing," she said, her southern upbringing making it come out sweet *thang.*

"And bring us both a blue plate special. That'll be fine — for now." Animal raised his eyebrows as if promising things to come.

Rather started to argue as the waitress moved away. "Goddammit, what did you do that for? I hate the sight of liver! Tastes like coagulated blood warmed over!"

Animal reached across the table and wrapped his hand around Rather's bandaged one. Even with the bandage, Animal's hand was bigger. He squeezed slowly until a look of pain appeared on Rather's face.

"Now you listen to me, asshole. If it weren't for

82

your fucking stupidity, I wouldn't be here wasting my time. Now don't give me any shit about anything, you hear? You just do whatever I tell you. No questions asked!"

As the big man increased the pressure on his hand, Rather's face turned white, then red, then white again. He took in several sharp breaths in quick succession before he managed to mutter, "Anything you say, Animal."

"Good. Let that be the end of it," Animal said, releasing his hand as the waitress arrived. Country music blared from the juke box.

"You fellas aren't from around here, are you?" she said, setting the plates on the table.

"Don't tell anybody," Animal said with the tone of a conspirator, "but we're from the government. Looking for a couple of young girls, secretaries, who stole some documents from the Defense Department in Washington. You haven't seen any strange girls around, have you?"

The woman opened her eyes wide. "You're putting me on, sugar. In Quinn's Inlet? Wouldn't exactly say this is a good place to hide. Ever'body knows ever'body here."

"Well, you're probably right, but they sent us here to look anyway. You'll let me know if you see anybody you don't know, won't you?"

The waitress grinned at him. "I would if I knew where you'd be staying, sugar."

"You know a motel we can get?"

"Only one around. The Botetourt Motel, about three miles down the road. Don't you worry. I'll find you if I see any strangers."

"I knew I could trust you," Animal said. "And oh,

83

could you tell me where I could find a used car dealer? We need to get a car they won't know."

"Max's Used Cars. It's about five miles from the motel. You turn left on Chapel Neck Road. If you can't find it, I'll be glad to show you. Later, when this place closes."

"Thanks," Animal said with a wink. "I'll call you. Maybe tomorrow."

"You be sure you do that, sugar."

Within the hour they were checked into the Botetourt Motel.

4

Two miles southeast of the motel and just on the outskirts of Quinn's Inlet, Jessie and Meredith were standing in the doorway of Dave's Paint and Body Shop watching the black Dodge pickup turn red. Dave had finally been persuaded by an offer of five hundred dollars in cold cash to do a quickie tape and spray job.

"Hope you don't mind if this isn't the best job you ever saw. Be better if I had more time for the taping," Dave said, working the sprayer back and forth in a smooth, even rhythm. He was a short man, about thirty, with a head of thin blond hair. He held a huge wad of chewing tobacco in his jaw.

Jessie forced her voice as low as it would go. "It's looking good," she said, satisfied, and put an arm around Meredith's shoulder.

"Don't like to do half-assed jobs, usually. Bad for the reputation, you know."

"We appreciate your doing this on short notice,"

Meredith told him, looking sweetly up at Jessie. "But, for all we know, Daddy is hot on the road behind us. He said he was going to take out a warrant to have me picked up."

Dave laughed the laugh of a conspirator. "Yep. Like I was telling you, me and mine ran away and got married too. Her old man wasn't too happy about it. Come after me with a shotgun. Said I never would amount to nothing. Don't guess I have by some folks' standards. But me and the wife been eatin' regular for twenty-five years. Raised four kids. Better than some folks I know do."

"Jessie and I want some kids some day," Meredith told him, looking up into Jessie's startled face. She had to bite her tongue to keep from laughing out loud as she saw the crimson flush of embarrassment begin at the line of Jessie's short hair and run down to her shirt. She knew Jessie would make her pay for that embarrassment later, but right now the teasing was for Jessie's own good. To get her mind off her nervousness. She wasn't sure yet that she looked enough like a man to pull this off.

Jessie shifted from one foot to the other and back again. "Yeah. Kids," she was finally able to croak. "Great idea."

"Got to have a job before you start thinking about kids though. Takes one hell of a pile of money, once kids start coming. You think they won't cost nothing, tiny things like that, but —" Dave gave a couple of guffaws, then spit a long stream of tobacco juice on the ground. "Diapers, clothes, shoes, braces." He was almost talking to himself as he worked. "They all add up. Lord, don't they add up."

Jessie was rocking back and forth on her boots,

heel to toe, and staring concentratedly at the ground. She said in her deepest voice, "Work the water, myself."

"Never liked that kind of thing," Dave said. "Seems like I can do just fine unless the wind comes up a bit and rocks the boat. Then I get seasick. Boy! Do I get sick. Just end up puking up my guts."

Jessie felt a surge of relief when she heard the rattle of an old farm truck behind them in the gravel driveway. The gray rocks crackled as the driver jumped down from the high cab seat. "Howdy, folks," a small black man said to them, tipping his hat to Meredith.

Dave looked up from his spraying. "Hello, Wash. What you up to?" he asked in a friendly tone.

"Was wondering if you happen to have a fan belt to fit my old truck here. Mine's about to break and I've got a load of crabs back there gonna kick off if I don't get them out of this sun before long."

"Look up in the shop, Wash. There's a bunch of them up on the shelf to the left."

"Pretty rickety old truck," Meredith said when the black man disappeared into the front of the building.

Jessie walked around to the truck bed, glad to have something to do besides stand around listening to Dave. The bed was full of bushel baskets, covered over with pieces of well-worn army surplus canvas. She lifted the edge of one and moved the basket top to one side. The basket was crammed to the brim with prime Jimmies — male blue crabs that measured six or more inches from shell tip to shell tip. She heaved an involuntary sigh.

"Don't let them big boys bite you, sonny," Wash's big voice boomed out behind her.

Jess dropped the basket top with a start. "Sorry, mister. I shouldn't have been fooling around in your things," she said apologetically.

"Never mind that. Just don't want you to lose a finger. Big ol' Jimmy can take a hunk out of you with his claws, he can."

"Yeah, don't I know it," she said, holding up her hands to show him the scars left by years of handling spunky blue crabs. "Lost a few hunks of fingers myself."

"You a waterman?" he asked.

"Been working for my daddy since before I was in high school. He's dead now though," she added faintly.

"Sorry to hear that," Wash said, throwing her an inquisitive look. "Help me with this fan belt?"

"Sure," she said, walking swiftly behind him toward the front of the truck.

Wash looked suspiciously toward the station bay where Meredith was still watching Dave paint the truck. "What's wrong with your truck? You wreck it? Don't look wrecked."

"No, it . . . we . . . ah."

"You got trouble, boy?"

"No! Well, yes. Ah, sort of. You might say that."

Wash laughed. "Well, do you or don't you?"

"It's not how it looks," she said glancing over at Meredith. "We left town . . . eloped, that is. And her daddy —"

"Stop right there, son. You don't owe ol' Wash no long explanations." He lifted up the rusty old truck

87

hood and leaned in over the engine. "Here. Hold this," he said, handing her the new fan belt.

He worked in silence for a few minutes. "Happens all the time, I guess. Pretty young girl. Handsome fellow. Pants get too hot for them to wait. Their folks think they're too fresh and innocent to get married. Hand me that wrench."

Jessie looked him over as she handed him the tool. Wash was gray across the short tight curls of his temples, but his face was unwrinkled. He had a timeless, solid look about him that made it impossible to tell his age. He wore a blue denim work shirt under bib overalls that were clean but not starched. His hands were calloused and scarred like those of someone who worked hard outdoors.

"You own your own boat?" she finally said, wanting to change the subject.

"Do now. It ain't a great big one, but it's mine. Worked on other folks' boats most of my life. Not many black men can buy their own boats."

"Guess not." She tried to remember if she had ever seen a black man in Maryland with his own boat. She could only think of one or two. "My dad owned his boat when he got ki . . . when he died."

Wash glanced back at Jessie. "Don't worry. Meddling around in other folks' business ain't exactly what I do best." He wiped his greasy hands on a rag.

Something about Wash made Jessie trust him. Maybe it was his eyes, which were more gray than brown, making them seem endless. Maybe it was because she had always wondered if black people felt as left out of the world as she did. "Somebody murdered my father," she said quietly, just for his ears. She was surprised to hear the words come out of her mouth.

Wash tightened up the last nut holding the new fan belt in place. He looked at Jessie again, this time in a peculiar, cautious way. "Something different about you, boy. You ain't like most of the white men I meet. Think maybe you ain't what you trying to seem."

High color flashed up into Jessie's cheeks. "Say," she stammered, "you wouldn't happen to be looking for a hand on your boat, would you? I need a job. I'd work as a culler or whatever you need."

He slammed the hood down on the truck and turned to face her, saying nothing for a few moments. Then: "Well, if you be needin' a job, I could use an extra hand. It's just me right now. I been looking for a helper, and you look strong and able."

"I know you don't even know me, but I'll work real hard."

Wash gave her a long, searching look. "Before you make up your mind," he said, "let me tell you something about old Wash. There are some people who say I'm kind of crazy. Sometimes I see things. I know things . . . that I ought not to know. Just seem to jump into my head."

"I don't understand what —" Jessie began. Then she stopped. The color drained out of her face. She had heard stories about people who had a sixth sense about things, who knew things they had no way of knowing, but she never really believed it. Something about Wash made her believe it was true. For him anyway.

"Nothing to be afraid of," Wash said. He looked

at her hard, then smiled kindly. "You think about that job. I'll be coming back through here in about an hour after I get my crabs marketed. Dave'll be through with your truck by then. We'll see."

After he left she told Meredith everything Wash had said.

By the time he got back they were ready to go with him.

5

"I don't understand any of this," Rather complained to Anamus after they checked into a room at the Botetourt Motel.

"You don't have to understand, you shithead," Anamus said, shucking out of his chinos. "All you have to do is follow my instructions. Got it?"

"I think we better start looking for the girl. She could be going God knows where while we fart around in this motel." Rather flopped down on one of the motel beds like a sulky, pouting child.

Animal kicked his huge Nikes off his feet and across the room with a thud. His shirt landed on the bed. In the dim light of the motel, he looked like a huge, hulking monster that had stepped out of a nightmare. The muscles in his chest and arms rippled as he shrugged his shoulders. He stared strangely at Rather before he stripped off his undershirt. "You're a thick-headed bastard, aren't you? We're going to perform a little experiment, Mr. Rather, before we do anything else. Actually you could think of it as a game. We can call it *Who's the Boss.*"

"I'm not doing anything except look for that girl,"

Rather said with bluster. His hand went suddenly for the pocket of his windbreaker.

In one long stride, Animal was on him. His large hand circled Rather's wrist easily and he pinned him to the bed with his large frame. "I'll take the gun, Mister," he said, extracting the .38 Police Special from Rather's pocket without releasing him. He leaned close to Rather's ear and spoke, almost in a whisper, "If you ever try to pull a gun on me again, I'll fill your asshole so full of lead the only way you can walk will be to waddle like a duck."

Animal rose carefully from the bed, taking the gun with him. Deliberately, he opened the revolving cylinder and let the bullets drop to the floor. Rather watched as each bullet hit the worn carpet and bounced crazily.

"Rather," Animal said, "I want you to practice being a duck. Get down here on the carpet and waddle for me." He pointed at the space in front of his large feet and pitched the empty gun on the bed.

"You're crazy!" Rather sat up and looked at him with bewildered eyes.

"You could be right," Animal said, and laughed. "Aren't most of us, after all? My craziness is just a little different from yours. Get down here and practice being a duck."

"You can't make me do that." Rather tried to laugh, but what came out was a choked whimper.

"For more than ten years, Mr. Rather, I have made a study of how to make people do the things I want them to do. You might say that it has become the passion of my life," Animal said serenely. "I have read everything that psychology and psychiatry have to offer on the subject. Don't doubt me. I can make you do what I want. I can turn you into whatever kind of creature I want you to be."

Rather opened his mouth to protest, but with one smooth motion Animal covered it with his hand. With the other, he closed Rather's nostrils, pinching so hard that no air could pass. He pushed him back on the bed, pinning him with his massive legs.

"You listen and you listen good. If you want to live, you'll do what I tell you," Animal said.

Rather struggled desperately, trying to pull away, moaning under Animal's hand. His chest heaved for air.

Slowly, with great deliberation, Animal twisted Rather's nose. "You *will* walk like a duck for me, won't you?" he said with false patience.

Rather kicked hard, trying to buck him off with the wild thrashing motions of a fear-crazed horse.

"God," Animal said, "you must be retarded."

It is possible to kill a man by breaking his nose and driving the cartilage back and upward through the unprotected brain tissue behind the nasal cavity, but Anamus didn't do that. Instead, he gave Rather's nose a sharp twist to the right, breaking it with a surgical precision which caused excruciating pain, but spared his life.

Rather's body relaxed suddenly. Blood trickled down his lip and into his mouth. His eyes rolled back in his head in sheer horror and anguish. Then, with all the precision of a ceremonial rite, Animal dipped his forefinger into the stream of blood and, with great care, wrote across Rather's forehead the word DUCK.

Animal stood by the bed, towering above him like a Gargantua. "It is a truism of power, *Mr.* Rather, that the human body can take just so much abuse before that wonderful protective organ, the brain, steps in and tells it to cooperate with whatever it is asked to do. There are no heroes, my friend. I have yet to meet anyone who cannot be made to do or be anything, if the pain and fear are sufficient. I have just changed you into my faithful servant, wouldn't you say, Mr. Rather? Now, get down on this floor and waddle like a duck!"

Griffin Rather slithered to the floor and walked on his haunches.

Chapter Six

1

Jessie and Meredith followed Wash's jiggling, jostling old farm truck for twenty miles before they reached his cottage just outside Quinn's Inlet. The final three miles cut through heavy woods and down a rutty, mud-colored road plagued with near axle-deep holes. Recent heavy rains had done little for its condition.

The house lay snug in a stand of tall pines laced

with gnarled vines of purple wisteria in full bloom. The cloying smell reminded Jessie of funeral flowers, too sweet to be enjoyed. The house itself was little more now than the logging shack it had started out as, but it was whitewashed clean and stood among the trees with dignity. Someone had added a screened front porch as a safeguard against hot summer days and nights.

Beside the house a chicken yard and coop were home to a couple dozen White Rocks and Rhode Island Reds. Two plump and sleek roosters swaggered around the periphery of the lot as the hens raced for the hen house with a cacophony of squawks at the sound of the trucks.

Wash stopped his truck beside the back door and motioned to Jess and Meredith as they pulled in behind him. "Come in and meet my wife," he called.

"You've got a nice-looking bunch of chickens," Meredith said, still watching the to-do in the poultry pen as she strolled across the yard.

"My wife's doing," he said. "I got a few rabbit hutches and a little garden over there." He pointed in the direction of the woods on the other side of the house.

"That you, Washington?" A heavy, jet-black woman opened the back door. She squinted at them from under her hand as she shaded her eyes against the sun.

"Me and some friends, Sarah. I brought some folks home. This uh . . . this fellow here is Jess and this is . . . uh . . . his wife. Meredith, I believe you said. Forgot to ask your last name. Don't matter anyhow."

"Name's Andrew . . . I mean, Anderson," Jessie stuttered. "Andrew Jessie Anderson. Glad to meet you."

Meredith stepped forward. "I'm Meredith Anderson. We come from Virginia. Just got married. Your husband said he might find work for Jessie."

Wash's wife glanced at the Maryland truck license, then looked quizzically at her husband. "I'm Sarah Jenkins," she said in a melodious voice. "You're welcome to come in."

Inside, the mixed smell of chlorine bleach and boiling collard greens was strong. As they walked through the kitchen, Sarah pointed toward two large vats on the stove and laughed. "I hope the smell won't knock you down. I've been washing and cooking all day. Have to boil Wash's work clothes or I can't ever get the smell of fish and crabs out of them."

They all walked through the living room which ran across the entire front of the house and onto the screened-in front porch. It was furnished with a porch swing, two rocking chairs and a table covered with oilcloth. Wash and Sarah took the swing. Wash motioned Jess and Meredith toward the chairs.

"We like to eat out here in the summertime," Wash said. "Nearly always get a little breeze. You can see the water through the trees if you look hard enough."

They leaned forward to peer through the trees. About three hundred feet in the distance they could see the gentle lap of the waves on the creek bank.

"That's Stutt's Creek. Wash and I don't own the waterfront land," Sarah told them. "But Rake

96

Johnson lets Wash use it. We give him a few eggs and some vegetables. Crabs and rabbits when he wants them."

The chains on the porch swing gave off a pleasant squeak as Wash and Sarah moved back and forth peacefully, the only sound for a while except for the birds chattering in the trees. The couple seemed content just to sit and rock.

"Well —" Jessie began hesitantly. She glanced at Meredith for help, but she seemed mesmerized by the quiet.

"Been thinking," Wash said suddenly. "You folks have to have some place to stay if you going to work with me, Jessie. All we got's one bedroom, but my brother's got an old place. Only about half a mile over from here if you walking through the woods. Longer by the road, 'course. My brother, he moved to Norfolk and hasn't lived in it in about five years. You could use it if you have a mind to."

Meredith didn't miss a beat. "We want to," she said.

"There's not much to that old house, Washington. It's about to fall in. White —" Sarah continued, "Nobody'd want to live in that old place."

"People can live anywhere when they're young." Then he added with a smile, "And all starry-eyed like these two. Besides, it wouldn't take too much to fix it up. They could work on it a little at a time."

"I don't know what their families would think," Sarah continued to protest to Wash as if Jess and Meredith were not there.

"Sarah, they've had a little trouble with their families. I'll explain it to you later," Wash said,

97

looking meaningfully at his wife, a do-be-quiet message in his eyes. "And we don't have to worry ourselves about that. Not now anyway."

She caught his drift. She knew Wash's uncanny intuition about things. "You're right I'm sure, sweetheart. Sometimes I forget how things used to be with us. We woulda lived in a tent just to be together." Then she added with a funny dreamy look, "Not that things are all that different now. Some things are just like they was when we was young."

Wash slapped his thigh, genuinely tickled by the implication. "Don't you wish, woman. Don't you wish. Oh, Jesus! I think your memory must be goin' on you!"

Jessie and Meredith looked at each other sheepishly.

"We don't want to make any trouble," Jessie said.

"No trouble, child. No trouble," Sarah said, standing up. "Come on with me, Meredith. We'll go kill us a hen for supper. I got plenty of greens and some squash in the garden. We better start getting to know each other if we're gonna be neighbors."

2

It was just after six that evening when Rather and Animal pulled into the parking lot of Max's Fine Used Cars. About a dozen late model cars surrounded a concrete block building that looked like an abandoned gas station. A string of uncovered light bulbs ran across the front and sides of the lot like a bunch of overgrown Christmas tree decorations. No one seemed to be around.

"Dammit! What do we need another car for?"
Rather bitched. "You act like we're going to take up
residence in this burg."

"We'll stay as long as we have to," Animal said
and glared at him. "Didn't I tell you to keep your
fucking mouth shut? Or would you like to find
yourself walking low to the ground again?"

Rather massaged his swollen nose gently and got
out of the car. His already round shoulders drooped
in a posture of defeat.

A sign over the door of the building read: NO
MUSS NO FUSS BUY YOUR NEXT CAR FROM
US NO MONEY DOWN NO CREDIT CHECK.

"Max seems real accommodating," Animal said,
and walked over to a light tan Oldsmobile Ciera.
White letters on the windshield proclaimed that it
was a 1985 model and sold for $9,995.00 Rather
followed wordlessly behind him.

They strolled around the lot looking at first one
car and then another. Rather occasionally kicked at a
tire, as if it gave him some inside information about
the car's condition.

"Got some real buys here," a voice behind them
said. "You fellows looking for a car?"

Animal turned to face the man. "What the hell do
you think we're looking for, a goddamned mule?"

"No-o, guess not," the man said with a little
nervous hitch. "What kind you looking for?"

"Something I won't have to put in the shop in
the morning. You got anything like that?"

"Everything on the lot carries a thirty-day
warranty. Limited, of course," he added.

"Limited to what?" Animal said. "The cigarette
lighter?"

99

"The power train."

"This great business empire belongs to you, I presume," Animal said.

"Guess it does." Max's adam's apple bobbed up and down as he spoke. He had the look of an aging hippy who hadn't realized that looking dirty and disheveled had gone out of style.

"Then I'll tell you just what I'm looking for, Max, and you better just hope you have it." Animal caught the man's wrist in a vise grip and squeezed hard. He didn't like hippies. They were all cowards. Left the country when there was a job to do. If it had been up to him, he would have taken a plank to their asses.

"What the hell? You're hurting me. Let me go." Max's face had taken on a pallid look and beads of sweat popped out on his upper lip just above his scrubby mustache.

Animal increased the pressure for a brief moment, rolling the thin bones back and forth, relishing the feeling of the power to break them before he suddenly let go.

"I am looking, Max," he said, in carefully measured words, "for a Dodge Ram pickup truck. I want a black one. Not a blue one. Late model. Not a new one. And I want it to have a camper shell on it. What do you think?"

Max looked at him strangely, then lowered his fear-filled eyes. "You can see I don't have anything like that," he said with a half-hearted gesture toward the cars on the lot.

"Yes, I can see that," he said. "But I would like for you to find one for me."

"Well, I don't know —" Max began.

"I would like for you to get on the phone right now and call all over this godforsaken county until you find one. Call all over this end of the state if you have to. You'll do it, unless you want to be a dead man. Do you understand?" Animal spoke with exaggerated precision.

"Come on, man," Max said, looking at him incredulously. "You gotta be crazy. What if nobody has a fucking truck like that? You're going to kill me because I can't find the kind of car you want? What kind of joke is this?"

Animal's huge hand snaked out to circle Max's wrist again. This time, lightly, almost lovingly. Slowly he ran his fingers and thumb up and down the man's arm.

"Unless you'd like to have your arms and legs broken, you'll get out in your very own car and you'll ride up and down the roads until you find one. Then you'll find me at the Botetourt Motel and tell me where it is. Understand?"

Max's face shot red with rage. "Look, man, you can't do this. This is a free country. I'll call the law. You see if I don't!"

Animal glared at the man. Then laughed loudly, showing his white shark-like teeth. "I don't think so, *man,*" he said with emphasis. "No, I don't think so."

He turned on his heel and walked slowly back toward the Buick. There was no need to hurry. None at all. His work was done for the day.

3

Before dark came, Wash took Meredith and Jessie

to his brother's house. The road from the highway, if it could indeed be called a road, was a twin to Wash's, only it was worse from years of neglect. Wash drove carefully through the woods toward the house, occasionally leaving the path to dodge deep ruts and blown down trees. NO TRESPASSING signs nailed to trees here and there were pockmarked with old buckshot wounds, tributes to the boredom of some hunter. They traveled a distance of perhaps a mile before they caught sight of the house through the trees.

Jessie felt pleasant surprise as a two-story farmhouse came into clear view. It was bigger than she had hoped. Clapboard siding peeped out from behind vigorous vines of English ivy, grown overly strong by years of freedom. The green metal roof was dimpled with rust, but seemed to be intact.

As soon as the truck came to a stop, Meredith jumped out to follow Wash to the front door. Jess hung back for a moment, looking fondly at the turn-of-the-century building. Houses were funny things; they either had character or they didn't. Like people. She supposed that it depended on how much love they had been given. This one seemed to radiate warmth. A lot of love had lived here. She felt an almost overwhelming affection for the place.

Her vision blurred. Unexpectedly, she missed her father, missed him terribly and longed for him to be here. There had not been much time for grief yet. But she knew it would come. Must come, if her hurt was ever to heal itself.

"Where are you, Jessie?" Meredith's voice sounded anxious and far away.

"I'm coming," she said, moving slowly toward the house. "Just woolgathering."

Jessie came through the door as Wash was saying, "In the old days, when this house was built, folks put the kitchen back away from the house so the house didn't get hot in the summertime from the cooking. Used to be, it was a separate building, but as you see, my brother connected it to the house with a hallway."

The hallway was about ten feet long, and narrow. The room it led to had a sink with a long-handled hand pump on one side and an ancient cast-iron wood stove on the other. Besides that, there was room for one small table.

"No electricity, Wash?" Meredith asked.

"Never has been. Guess you could get some put in, if you want to spend the money." As they walked back through the hallway to the main house, Wash added, "There ain't no indoor plumbing either. The old outhouse out back still works though." He laughed as if he had told a joke.

"Holy shit," Meredith muttered, not intending to pun.

"You can see now why Sarah thought you might not want to live over here. And that's why when my brother moved to Norfolk, he just left this old place and didn't try to sell it."

"I think it's terrific," Jessie said. "Has it got any kind of heat?"

"Fireplaces," Wash said. "One down here in the living room and one upstairs in one of the bedrooms. Guess you could use this room we're standing in for a dining room or whatever you want to make it. That is, if you still want the place after seeing it."

"If you're sure it would be all right with your brother, we'll move in right now. Got a couple of sleeping bags in the truck. We'll be real happy with it," Jessie said.

"It's yours then." Wash handed her the key. "I brought along a kerosene lantern so you'd have some light. Just in case you decided to stay."

"Guess you thought we might," Jess said, smiling.

"Had a hunch," Wash said. "Be ready to start crabbing with me tomorrow?"

"Just tell me what time."

"Be at my house just before sunup."

"You got it, friend. You got it," Jessie said happily. "It'll do my heart and soul good to get back on the water."

4

Hours later, Jessie and Meredith sprawled out on sleeping bags in the middle of the bedroom floor. Moonlight streamed in through an open window, bathing their naked bodies. Somewhere in the distance, a hound brayed mournfully at the moon, the sound so eerie it sent cold chills through Meredith, making her shiver.

"You look exhausted," Jessie said, reaching for her protectively. She moved her hand up and down the silky furrow of Meredith's spine for a few moments, then she cupped her buttocks in her ample hand and pulled her decisively into the contours of her own body.

"This is the first time I've felt safe since I saw

those men," Meredith said. "God! Finally a place we can call our own. It feels wonderful even without electricity and plumbing!" She snuggled so the length of her body fit perfectly with the ins and outs of Jessie's.

"I've never felt anything as wonderful as your body," Jessie whispered. "Who could have known that anything could feel like this?"

"Remember when we used to wrestle with each other when we were kids?" Meredith laughed softly. "I loved touching you then. I used to deliberately pick arguments with you, so you would finally grab me and we would roll around on the ground, fighting."

"You really are bad," Jessie said, gazing at her face in wonder. "You never told me that. I thought you hated me then." She stroked Meredith's cool smooth cheek, then traced the outline of her eyes and shell-like ears with gentle fingers. Slowly and deliberately, she ran her tongue along the curves of Meredith's body, moving downward to circle her nipples, then her navel, and finally to the center of her pleasure, where she stayed until she felt her shiver and heard her cry out.

Meredith's hands found Jessie's cropped hair and pulled her mouth up to her own. Her tongue went over Jessie's lips like a flitting butterfly. When Jessie's tongue caressed the inner velvet of her cheeks, she pressed hard against her teeth, bringing pain and burning sweetness to them both.

Warm moisture spread through Jessie's thighs. She was racked suddenly with a craving that skyrocketed into her brain, sending her body out of control and pulsing against Meredith. Her heart pounded against her ribs and her breath came in ecstatic gasps.

Meredith opened her legs to pull Jessie's thigh between them, thrusting rhythmically against her hardness.

Jessie moved her hand between their bodies, trying to touch Meredith's silky explosive mound with her fingers, but Meredith's thighs were closed too powerfully, blocking entrance.

Meredith pulled her mouth free, desperately seeking air; then she buried her face in Jessie's shoulder and, as if through some primitive reflex, she began a rhythmic sucking on her skin that paced perfectly the thrusting of her hips. Her thrusts, which had been quick and shallow, became deep and driving. She pushed again and again, harder and harder, until she suddenly stopped at the height of her movement and trembled.

"Oh, Jesus! Oh, God," she murmured as she arched her back one last time, then fell back, totally soft and relaxed.

Little by little her breathing slowed. Jessie had not moved. "You didn't know I was so greedy, did you?" Meredith said finally, with a smile.

Jessie smiled back. "Is that what it is?"

"No, it's because you're so damned sexy. That's what it really is. Touching you turned me on so much I couldn't wait." She put her fingers lightly on Jessie's mouth.

Jessie grinned appreciatively and gave her a devilish look. Playfully she began to lick Meredith's fingers, one by one.

"Ummmm . . ." Meredith murmured.

"Feel good?" Jessie asked. "You like this?" She took her hand and brought Meredith's palm to her mouth, licking it with light darting motions. Then she worked her way down to her wrist, licking lightly first, then kissing.

She had begun on the inside of her arm when Meredith groaned, "God, woman, you're turning me on again."

This time Jessie found easy access to her warmth with her fingers. "That's exactly what I had in mind," she told her.

5

Wash's boat was expertly tied at the end of the dock off the property that fronted his own land. It was a forty-foot Chesapeake deadrise, painted white from front to back with a glossy enamel except below the water line, where it was coated with rust-red copper-bottom paint. Without the copper paint, which was toxic to marine life, the bottom of the boat would soon be covered with barnacles which would impede the boat's movement through the water.

Jessie had left Meredith, still sleeping, long before dawn, but she found Wash already at work when she arrived at the pier.

She hustled quickly on board to help him stow the two large boxes of menhaden which they would use to bait the crab pots. As usual, the smell of the greasy fish assaulted her nostrils.

Wash laughed when he saw her wrinkle her nose. "Bunkers always stink, don't they?" he said, using the local name for menhaden. "Crabs never seem to mind though. I guess ever'thing on God's earth's good for somethin'."

Jessie grinned at him, observing that Wash had somehow developed the habit of seeing good in everything. It was a quality she liked. "The more they stink, the better the crabs like 'em," she said. "My dad —"

Wash looked at her as if he understood, then said, "Jessie, if your dad was as smart a waterman as I suspect he was, then he knew enough to leave his bunkers out over night. Let 'em get good and warm and stinky. Young fellas keep 'em cold, but they don't catch crabs near as good."

It took thirty minutes to maneuver the boat out of the creek and out into the bay where Wash had set his pots. They didn't see the first buoy until almost dawn. With skill honed by years of experience, Wash moved the boat into perfect position so that he could grab the bullet-shaped float swiftly with a hook mounted on a long stick. He reached easily for the buoy rope and hauled the two-and-a-half-foot square wire-mesh trap on board, hand over hand. As he brought it aboard, he turned it upside down and gently shook the crabs toward the bottom. Almost in the same smooth motion he handed the crab pot back to Jessie.

There was nothing mentally taxing about crabbing; Wash simply had to keep his eyes and hands working together and he could let his mind wander wherever it would take him. "Jessie," he said, "I know I said I wasn't interested in your business, but if you don't mind me asking, you got any ideas about what happened to your dad?"

"Not for sure. I think he was in some kind of

108

trouble though," Jessie said, then added, "Although he wasn't the kind to get into trouble that I knew of."

With expert hands, she took the pot Wash handed to her, released the hook that held the top closed and shook the crabs into the bottom of the boat. They scurried for cover as they fell around the crabbers' booted feet.

"Don't overload the bait well," Wash said, watching Jessie stuff a handful of bunkers into the small wire compartment that would rest on the floor of the bay when the crab pot was thrown back in the water. "Long as there's enough to give 'em a good smell, that's all you need."

With one smooth motion, she flipped the pot upright and back into the water. Wash had meanwhile moved the boat up to the next pot and was bringing it on board.

"I'm really grateful to you for this job," Jessie said, stuffing bait into the next pot.

"Glad to have the help. And the company. I get to talking to myself when I work alone. Or to the sea gulls," Wash laughed.

Jess glanced behind the boat at the flock of gulls that trailed them, watching for pieces of old bait to fall out of the pots as Wash brought them on board.

"No need to worry unless they start to talk back," she teased him.

"Any notion who might have killed him? Your dad, I mean."

"Who knows? Some people didn't like him very much. He was pretty straitlaced for a waterman. It's kinda spooky though. Two men came to see him at the house the night before he was killed."

"Nobody you know, I take it." Wash handed back another crab pot.

"Never seen either one of them before. Or since," she started to add, then remembered the man at the rest stop. "I'm pretty sure I have seen one of them since, though. He came after Meredith and me with a shotgun the other night, but we — we managed to get away from him. He seemed to think we had something real valuable. Meredith thinks it was probably drugs he was after, but I can't imagine my dad being involved with anything like that."

They were working in easy rhythm, getting the hang of each other's movements, so that pots were coming up and going back into the water evenly.

"Looks like we're gonna get a pretty good mess of crabs today," Wash said. "Never did talk about pay, did we?"

"I figure you'll do me right."

"How's a thirty-seventy split, after gas and bait? With the house thrown in for nothin'."

"Fine by me. We can make out easy on that."

"How'd you meet your —" Wash coughed. "How'd you meet Meredith?"

Jessie blushed. "Went to school together. She lived just down the road from us." Jessie hesitated, then began haltingly, "Wash, there's something I have to tell you about —"

"You don't need to tell ol' Wash nothing. Don't care much about what folks do — as long as they's good folks and does good things for other folks. Ever'body's a little different. Different makes 'em interesting. Be kinda borin' if ever'body's the same."

Jess smiled gratefully. She knew that her sense of

110

him had been right. She could trust him to understand.

Fifty or sixty gulls were following the boat, wheeling through the air and screaming back and forth to each other. It was getting harder to hear above their noise and the clamor of the boat engine.

"How many crab pots you workin'?" Jessie yelled to Wash.

"About three hundred. All I could handle by myself, but I thought we'd start addin' some more, if it's all right with you. Maybe a hundred or so. What you think?"

"Be fine with me. Dad and I worked five or six hundred. Sometimes more. Two people can do that many."

"What kinda trouble you think your daddy might have been in," Wash asked, "if it didn't have to do with drugs?"

"To tell you the truth, I don't have a clue. All I know is he was on his way to talk to the sheriff the day he was murdered."

"Just wonderin'," Wash said. "I think there might be something funny goin' on around here. If I was you, I'd keep my eyes open."

Jessie looked up sharply. "That's what I intend on doing. What do you think's going on?"

"Can't say for sure. Just that some crabbers got more money than they ought to have lately, the way crabs has been runnin' so scarce." Wash hesitated. "Jessie, you want me to put out the word that you needing money bad?"

"Would you do that, Wash?"

"I will if you want me to. But you got to promise

111

me to be real careful. For now, let's just get these old rascals in the boat so we can get on back home. Some women I know gonna be lookin' for our ugly faces."

By the time they finished and sold their day's catch, it was just past three in the afternoon.

Chapter Seven

1

The month of April vanished, bringing May and its promise of new birth. Red-winged blackbirds courted one another shamelessly in the river marshes, and long-necked gray herons began to patrol the creek banks, searching for newly-hatched minnows.

It was near-idyllic time for Jessie. Long days of hard work on the bay with Wash provided ample time for reflection and for grief, so that by the time the daffodils gave way to tulips, some sense of balance and peace had come back to her life.

Meredith fared a little less well. Not long after the restoring and painting of the house was underway, she picked up a flu bug that left her sneezing and sniffling for weeks. Sarah stuffed her full of chicken soup and aspirin and insisted bed rest was the only cure. Meredith would have none of it. For a while she spiked a fever at night, but managed to paint and hammer and hang Sarah's hand-me-down curtains during the day anyway. By the middle of May, her cold had disappeared and the house once again had a people-live-here look. Stubborn weeds and vines that had grown accustomed to having free reign in the yard lost a major battle to Jessie's weekend and evening persistence.

It would have been easy for them to forget all that had happened, but Jessie kept a watchful eye on the people at the dock.

2

Things might have stayed peaceful if, on May 18, Jessie had not mailed a letter to Sybil Ekstrand in Pliney Point. As luck would have it, the starter went bad on Wash's truck so he asked Jessie to take hers to the dock to sell the crabs that afternoon. It was that or lose the whole day's catch to the summer heat. It just made sense to go on to town while they were out.

Jessie dropped Wash off at the NAPA parts place to pick up a new starter. He needed to get some other things Sarah wanted, he told her, while she drove on down to the dock to sell their catch.

She became aware of the man watching her as she counted the money the dock manager had paid her. The man was perched on a piling at the end of the pier, tamping his pipe and looking at her. Suddenly he stood up, stretched, and walked in her direction.

"What's on your mind, buster?" she said as he approached. She rubbed her chin self-consciously as men often do when their newly grown beards itch.

He stuck his pipe into his too-wide mouth and fingered the stem lovingly. His eyes were tiny little pig slits and his sweat-stained chambray work shirt smelled of fish.

"Been watchin' you, boy," he said with a grin that sparkled in the sunlight with gold inlays. "Been waitin' to catch you alone, so I could talk to you."

"That a fact?" Jessie said, starting to turn away.

"Wait a minute," he said quickly. "Listen, I asked some folks about you. Hear tell you working for that crazy nigger. White boys like yourself can do better."

Jessie eyed him, then smiled a little. "Ain't no business of yours if I work for the devil."

"You don't need to be so damned touchy. Name's Redman. Hap Redman. I work for the man that owns this dock. A partner, you might say. I hear you want to make some *real* money. I can tell you how."

Jessie filled in the blanks in her mind. This could be the kind of offer somebody had made her father. "What makes you think I need more money than I'm gettin'?"

"Ever'body needs more money. Besides that, I hear you livin' in an old run-down house ain't even

115

got plumbing. Even niggers won't live in it. I know you want better than that for that pretty wife of yours."

Jessie didn't reply with words, but swallowed pointedly and ran her fingers nervously through her short dark hair.

"Yeah, I thought so," Hap said. "I had one of my men do a little checking on you." Then he leveled his finger at Jessie. "I can tell you ain't stupid, boy. And I can fix you up."

"What have I gotta do?" Jessie asked, then added, "I don't want any trouble with the law."

Hap looked at her for a long moment. "Everything connected with big money is a little illegal, one way or another. How would you like to bring in a thousand dollars most every time you go on the water?"

Jessie felt her heart quicken, but she fought hard to keep a disinterested expression on her face. "Nothing that pays that good's likely to be legal, now is it? Don't think I want to risk gettin' my ass thrown in jail, but I'll give it some thought," she said, and headed for her pickup truck.

"You do that. You think on it, but not too long," he called after her. "This offer ain't gonna last forever. And be sure you meet me at Fleet's Cafe tonight about eight to talk about it. That is, if you want to see that little wife of yours has everything she wants. And," Redman added, "if you want to see her stay as pretty as they say she is now."

Jessie looked back sharply, trying to judge whether Redman had made a joke or a threat. His face gave no clear sign of his intent. "I guess since you put it like that," she said, "I'll be there."

3

The word had been passed from Dave to Max to Animal that a young man and woman had been in a mighty hurry to have their black truck painted red. Dave was a nice enough fellow normally and might have kept his mouth shut about the hurry-up paint job, but he did, after all, need things for his kids. When Max put out the word that there was two hundred dollars in it for a truck just like he wanted, Dave had stepped forward with the information that he had seen one. Only trouble was, he didn't know what had happened to it after he painted it. But Griffin Rather had spotted it the minute it pulled in to the wharf at Quinn's Inlet.

4

Later that afternoon Jessie found Meredith trying to wash clothes in a large metal wash pot in the yard behind their house. A huge fire was blazing underneath the pot, bringing the water to a healthy boil. Meredith had put in a half a box of soap and was stirring as best she could with a mop handle.

"Double, double, toil and trouble, fire burn and cauldron bubble." Meredith was sing-songing the lines from Macbeth she had learned in high school as she circled the pot, trying to stay out of the smoke, wiping the sweat from her eyes. She turned around to find Jessie watching with an expression of amusement.

"And how long have you been standing there, smartybutt?"

"Just long enough to find out you really are a witch. I always did think so. Why don't you just put the clothes in the washing machine?"

"Ha-ha, you're so funny. Just keep running your mouth and you'll find yourself sleeping on the couch tonight."

Jessie grinned and grabbed her from behind, swinging her in a full circle. "Don't be cruel, darlin'. That's a fate worse than death. Besides, we don't have a couch."

"You're so full of shit, Jessie. One of these days you're going to get yours." She swung the mop handle backward over her head as if to hit her.

"I don't have time to get mine right now, but I do need to talk to you. Can you turn off the washing machine for a minute?"

Meredith put her hands on her hips in mock exasperation, then headed for one of the lawn chairs Jessie had rescued from the county dump. "Sarah says soaking clothes is good for them if you don't —"

Jessie stopped her with a kiss and then sat on the ground at her feet. "I've got a meeting with a man tonight. Says I can make a lot of money working for him."

"You want to quit working for Wash?"

"No, no, no! Remember Wash told me a while back that something strange was going on around here? People making a lot of money. I think this may be it."

"You still think this has something to do with your dad's death?"

"I don't know. But it might. I'm not much on playing detective, but I think I have to do this, just in case. Besides, you were the one who said we had

118

to do everything we could to find out what happened."

"I know that," Meredith said in a low voice. She put her hand under Jessie's chin and solemnly tilted her face up. Then she grinned from ear to ear. "And I'm going with you to your meeting. After all, I am your *wife*! Let's get ready to go! The laundry can wait."

As they rose to go into the house, Jessie glanced behind her. She couldn't shake the feeling she was being watched.

5

As they entered Fleet's Cafe that evening, a rain-freshened breeze blew off the bay and smelled so wonderfully sweet that it was hard for Jessie or Meredith to believe that this night could be about anything other than dining on fresh-caught seafood.

Hap Redman sat in the back booth next to the jukebox, filling his pipe from a brown leather pouch, his slit-like eyes darting around the room. Beside him sat a giant of a man with bulging muscles and piercing eyes. When Hap spotted Jessie he waved her toward him.

"Here we go!" Jessie muttered under her breath.

Meredith stood perfectly still for a second of posing before she followed Jessie. Her china blue eyes were wide, taking in the scene. Her long blonde hair was pulled back and tied with a powder pink scarf that hung down to her waist. She wore a hot pink off-the-shoulder blouse pulled low and jeans tight enough to belong to someone a size smaller. Her earrings were round and gold and hung to her shoulders.

Redman looked her up and down as she approached the table. "Well," he said, "you must be the wife. You ain't bad looking. I heard that."

"My name's Meredith, sugar," she said, giving her chewing gum a couple of good wallops. "Meredith Anderson. What's yours?" She smiled sweetly and leaned close, almost brushing him with her breasts.

"Sit down, Meredith," Jessie said, pushing her gently into the booth. She slouched her own long body down across from Redman.

"Name's Hap Redman. This here's Walter Anamus. Business partner of mine."

Animal extended his huge paw to Jessie for a handshake, but said nothing.

"Don't recall inviting you to come along, Miz Anderson, but I guess it's all right. You play a part in this too, in a way. Sissy," Hap yelled to the waitress, "bring us four beers."

Redman played with his pipe until the drinks came. They all listened attentively as on the jukebox Dolly Parton belted out a song about a coat her mother made out of rags, but both men stared at Meredith all the while. Redman poured his Pabst slowly down the side of the frosted mug and took a long drink before he said, "We might as well get down to business, don't you think, Mr. Anamus?"

"This is your party, Mr. Redman," Anamus said dryly.

"Jessie, I'm prepared to set you up with your own boat. I'll buy your crab pots, license, everything you need to get started. What do you say to that?"

Jessie narrowed her eyes and pulled her body up

straight. Before she answered, she made a set of wet circles on the table with her beer bottle. "What would you want to do that for? Don't make much sense," she said solemnly.

Hap grinned his dazzling gold grin and nodded. "Oh, it's not that unusual. I got ten or twelve boys workin' for me. I take a cut out of the catch. Mostly, I like to help fellas kinda down on their luck. Give 'em a hand, you might say. It might sound funny to you, but that way I can make money and not have to work so hard."

Meredith leaned forward and fussed with her blouse sleeves. "Just how much *could* Jessie make doing that, Mr. Redman? He said you mentioned an awful big figure this morning. A thousand dollars a day?"

"Well, he could make that. You know, dependin' on how hard he's willing to work."

"Hell," Jessie said, standing up as if to leave, "I can make that now if I want to work night and day! And crabbin' after dark is illegal. Thanks, buster, but no thanks!" She started to move out of the booth.

Meredith grabbed at Jessie's shirt sleeve and smiled nervously at the tall man. He was looking a hole through Jessie's face. "Wait, honey," Meredith said, "don't be so impatient."

Redman laughed. "I don't mean that, young fella. Sit down. Hard work can mean a lot of things besides long hours. Anyway, I'm sure you'd do most anything for this little lady here." He winked broadly at Meredith.

"Yeah? Suppose you tell me exactly what you do mean." Jessie took a drink from the brown bottle and looked hard at Redman.

"All you have to do is occasionally pick up a special package, out there on the water. And bring it to me, of course."

"Drugs? You want me to bring in drugs?" Jessie asked cautiously.

"Could be guns, honey, but for that kind of green . . ." Meredith giggled, brushing affectedly at her hair and chewing vigorously on her gum.

Anamus spoke a second time. "Better you don't know what. In fact, the less you know the better, but you can make a lot of money. How about it?"

"I don't know," Jessie said.

"He'll do it, Mr. Redman. Won't you, Jessie?" Meredith said impatiently with a touch of wildness in her voice. "I'm sure these men wouldn't ask you to do anything . . . dishonest, honey."

Jessie looked at her curiously. "Well, if she wants me to that much . . ."

"Then it's settled. I'll be in touch with you in a few days," Redman said, waving for the waitress. "Sissy! Bring us four of them Seafood Platters."

Animal stood up, towering over the table. "Not for me, Redman, I've had all I want," he said. "I'll talk to you later, but I'm sure Mr. Anderson here is just the man we've been looking for." He headed for the door.

6

Jessie and Meredith lay quietly in each other's arms watching the moonlight and listening to the frogs sing their lonely spring song.

"Well," Jessie said when she could stand it no

longer, "I guess we're gonna find out what Redman's up to now whether we want to or not. How did I do? Did I overdo it?"

"You were divine, Miss J, just divine!" Meredith punched at the ticklish spot on her ribs.

"Oh, get serious! Do you think he bought it? Did I act hesitant enough? I was trying not to look too eager."

"God, I was planning to kick your ass if you acted any more hesitant. I thought you'd never tell him yes!"

"Meredith, there's something serious I want to say to you," Jessie said, deliberately changing the subject. "Don't you say anything. Just listen."

Meredith waited for her to continue.

"I want to tell you how sorry I am that, well, that I wouldn't live with you before. I've been so selfish — and scared, I guess. It was just that I thought I had all the time in the world to do everything I wanted to do. And that somehow you'd always be there."

"You don't have to do this, sweetheart," Meredith whispered.

"Meredith, please let me." She reached for her hand and drew a deep breath. "These last few weeks, since Dad died, and after I thought we were both goners for sure at that rest stop, I've begun to realize how very precious life is and how short it can be. And how you have to take the really good things you have when you have them and not put off the caring for them and about them until sometime in the future. Am I making any sense?"

"Infinite sense."

"I'm going to care for you as hard as I can every

single minute of the day for the rest of my life, no matter what."

Meredith didn't speak for fear of breaking the spell.

Jessie was quiet for a long while, then she leaned on her elbow. "And listen, Meredith, I want to ask you something. That night before we left Pliney Point you made a crack about me liking to stomp around in my white boots at the bar in Baltimore. You remember that?"

"Why?" Meredith asked, not acknowledging that she had said it.

"Well, we only went that one time. And I was wondering . . . did I embarrass you?"

Meredith laughed. "Jesus, no! Every woman there was drooling over you. Those cute little dimples and that cleft chin! Thought I'd have to handcuff you to the table to keep some of those women from walking off with you! I was proud to be with you."

Jessie sighed, pleased with her response. Reminiscing, she continued, "Remember how we got there? How you found that book in that women's bookstore that told where all the gay bars in the country are? God, I was scared to death to go!"

"I remember," Meredith said with a smile in her voice. "And do you remember that great big woman they had at the door? How she looked us over to make sure we looked right before she'd let us in? *Members Only* the sign said."

"Yeah, what do you think she was looking for?" Jessie asked innocently.

The remark caused Meredith to sit up straight in the bed and howl with laughter.

Suddenly Jessie was laughing too. Tears streamed

down her face, not because she knew what was funny, but because the laughter was contagious. "Well, what do you think it *was*, Meredith? What was it? Tell me! I'm serious!"

Meredith hooted again and began to hiccup from laughing. Finally she raised her hand and begged, "Stop, Jessie, oh please, please, stop! Someday I'll explain it to you — if you ever grow up!"

The tension of the day wound down a little for each of them as they wiped the tears from their eyes. Then Jessie took Meredith's face in her hands and kissed away the last of the wetness.

"Oh, God, I love you so much, Meredith. I hope we're doing the right thing. If anything happens to you . . ."

"Nothing is going to happen. God looks after lovers. Don't you know that?"

Meredith took Jessie's delicate breast in her mouth and caressed it with her tongue until she felt the nipple stiffen. Slowly and deliberately she moved downward to the downy space above the dark, pointed arrow of her pubis. Tiny kisses, wet with passion, fanned the fire until Jessie groaned and arched upward, pressing herself against the punishing, promising mouth, seeking more and finding it.

Quickly, with a deftness born of familiarity, Meredith moved her body to give easy access to the throbbing moistness between her own legs.

"So good, so good," Meredith murmured as she felt Jessie's tongue caress the satin of her inner thighs, then enter her warmth, moving tenderly, bringing the welcomed sensation.

Jessie reached for Meredith's breasts with both hands, stroking them over and over her own stomach until Meredith cried out with pleasure, and moved harder and faster against her mouth.

She didn't give Meredith that pleasure long before she shifted her weight, bringing a vague protest when she moved her to her back. She ran her hands all over Meredith's body as if she couldn't get enough of her, feeling the weight of her breasts, her hardened nipples and the roundness of her bottom.

Meredith took Jessie's hand and guided it between her legs, forcing her fingers into the velvety moistness there and arching her hips instinctively to take them in, shuddering at their entry.

Jessie moved again to lie nearly on top of her. Her other hand slid under her to cup her bottom and draw her close so that she could meet the thrust of her hips. As the aching tension began to build, Meredith dug her fingers in Jessie's shoulders, clutching tightly, holding the magical moment steady as if she feared it would be lost.

Jessie firmly matched the pace with her own thrusts, so that they flowed as one body in a rhythm as old as the universe until the climax shattered them both and left them full and contented.

Before she slept, Jessie folded Meredith into her arms and whispered in her ear, "You must be right about God and lovers, sweetness. She must care a heck of a lot to give us anything as wonderful as that."

Meredith wrapped her warm body around Jessie's and made a noise like a cat's purr.

Chapter Eight

1

The day Jessie's letter arrived, the topic of conversation at Sybil's Bar and Grill was another dead body. Sheriff Todd had stopped in for a mid-morning cup of coffee on his way back from picking up an autopsy report at the county morgue.

"Nobody from around here," the sheriff said to Sybil. "The coroner figures he'd been in the water four or five days. Fish and crabs did a pretty good number on him before he floated. Had big heavy chains wrapped around him like the kind you see at a wharf."

"Any ID?" Kenny Westerlake asked him.

"A wallet, but the papers in it were pretty faded out by the water. Name might have been Italian. Looked like D'Angelo or D'Ah-something or other."

"You think this is connected with the Andrews killing?" Kenny asked.

"Could be. Only I don't know what the connection is."

"Speaking of Andrews, I got a letter from Jessica this morning," Sybil said, as she walked over to open the cash register. "I stuck it in here until I had time to sit down and read it. Got busy for breakfast this morning."

"I'll get us more coffee." Kenny moved back behind the bar near Sybil and started drawing coffee from a big gray urn. "Todd, you know a fella named Micky Bates? Young fella. Real light blond hair. A clean-cut military look about him."

"Doesn't ring a bell," Todd said.

Kenny set three brimming coffee mugs on the table and sat down. "Took my boat over to the Bay Marina this morning to have a little work done on the engine. Been running rough. Anyway, Jim Matteson — you know Jim, runs the marina — Jim's got this young fella Bates over there pumping gas, selling bait and doing odd jobs. Never seen him before, so I asked Jim where he came from. He said he just pulled up one day in a big Sea Ox and said he was looking for work, so Jim hired him right there on the spot."

"Nothing odd about that, is there? Lots of college

kids think they want to work around water in the summer."

"No, not that, but Jim said that first day Bates came he had this older fella with him he said was his uncle. Said the guy looked like he might be drunk or zonked out on drugs."

"Don't tell me he was a dark-looking man. Maybe Italian?"

Kenny laughed. "It does sound like too much of a coincidence, doesn't it? But that's what he said. Said he thought it was sorta funny, the man being so dark and the kid so blond. And —"

"And, he hasn't seen the dark fella since. Right?"

"Right. Guess you think I'm trying to play Mike Hammer."

Todd leaned forward to pat Kenny on the arm. "Be worth looking into. I'll go over and talk to Jim. The boy too."

"Want to know what Jessie had to say?" Sybil asked, as she settled herself back down at the table with the letter. "You'll be interested in this, Sheriff. You know that Tomkins girl? The one that's been missing? She's with Jessie. I'm not surprised though. They were such good friends."

"Meredith Tomkins? I heard from one of her brothers that she'd left. Not exactly an official complaint. I think he was just pissed that nobody was ironing his shirts and cleaning up after him anymore. The mother's pretty crazy, I think."

"Jessie says they're fine and she's working on a crab boat for some man. Doesn't say what Meredith is doing. She wants to know if there's any news on her father."

"Well, that's interesting, but I've got things to do," Todd said, swallowing the rest of his coffee in one big gulp as he stood up to leave. "Listen," he said as he put on his hat, "is there a return address on that letter? I've got some personal things of Andrews that were on his body. Jessie left before I could give 'em to her. Maybe you'd send 'em along, if you're going to write, that is."

"Yeah, there is, Sheriff. And the postmark says Quinn's Inlet. They didn't go far."

2

Melrose Todd had been a police detective in Baltimore until June of 1983, and he had a lot of experience with interrogation. He'd been a fifteen-year man working on twenty when he got a bellyful of city violence and vice and moved his wife and two kids to the country. Little by little, puttering around in his garden in the evenings and fishing on weekends had drawn some of the pus out of his soul.

"No," Todd said in answer to Bates' challenge, "you don't have to answer any questions if you don't want to, 'cause you're not charged with anything. And that means you *don't* have the right to an attorney."

"Be better if you'd just cooperate with us," said the woman in the crisp green skirt and white blazer. She had been in town less than three hours. "That way, we won't have to go around looking for something to charge you with and we can get this over this morning so you won't be late for work."

Her name was Billie Robinson. She was an agent

with the Federal Bureau of Investigation in Washington, D.C. She knew who Micky Bates was. He was Marvin Brennerman, formerly of the U.S. Marine Corps. Jim Matteson over at the marina had handed over to the sheriff several things that Bates had handled, and Robinson had come down from Washington in a big hurry when Todd had sent Bates' fingerprints in on a routine check.

"What can I tell you?" Bates asked. "I'm just working at the marina for the summer, between semesters." He sat stiff between Todd and Robinson with his hands clasped behind his back, feet spread a step or two apart. The fluorescent light shone like a floodlight on his pale blond hair. It made him look about eighteen and he knew it. It was that look of innocence that had made him so valuable as a Mafia gun.

"You *are* sure this man is your uncle?" Robinson asked, holding up the photograph of the face of a corpse sent over by the coroner's office. "Jim Matteson identified him as the man you were with the first day you came to the marina."

"That's my uncle. I told you it was. By marriage. Married my old man's sister just a couple months ago." Bates-Brennerman focused on some imaginary spot on the far wall. The only movement of his cold blue eyes was a slight, barely noticeable, tick of his right eyebrow. Todd was used to looking for such signs during questioning. Robinson lit a Marlboro and pushed up the sleeves of her blazer. "Where's your aunt live? You don't sound like you live around here. Sound more like a Yankee."

"My family's from Chicago. I came down here to go to school. Military school," Micky said.

131

"Nothing personal between you and your uncle? No bad feelings? Maybe something about your aunt?" Robinson knew it was all bullshit. She had a whole file on Brennerman.

"I didn't care much for him. He was drunk the whole time he was here."

"How did he happen to be down here? Away from Chicago, I mean," Robinson asked, still playing along.

Todd watched for the eyebrow to twitch. He thought he smelled coffee from the outer office. The morning shift had arrived.

"Just passing through. Guess my aunt told him where I was. How many times do you want to hear it?" Bates said, losing patience. "He came in that afternoon. I took him over to the marina with me. We had dinner that evening and he left. I thought he went back to Chicago!" This time he glanced over at Billie Robinson to see her reaction. He hadn't meant to raise his voice.

Robinson slowly stubbed out her half-smoked cigarette in the ashtray on the long table that filled the interrogation room. She avoided Micky's eyes. "Don't guess you know who killed him?" she asked, not looking up. It can take a long time to put out a cigarette when you try hard.

"No. I do *not* know who killed him," Micky answered, emphasizing each word individually.

"Didn't think you would," Robinson said, tapping a fresh cigarette on the table.

They all sat silent for a time as Robinson made a ritual of lighting the new cigarette. She looked straight into Brennerman's eyes through the flame

132

from the gold-plated lighter as if she could read his thoughts. He shifted his weight on the chair.

Todd glanced at his watch. Five-thirty. Dragging this suspect out of bed for questioning was a technique Billie Robinson had suggested. Something about the early morning hours making people more vulnerable. Maybe it took a while to get the defensive juices really pumping after sleep.

"Well," Billie said finally, "I guess that's all we need to ask you. We really didn't think you'd know much. You can go for now."

"What do you mean, for now?" Bates-Brennerman asked.

"Don't get any notions about visiting your momma in Chicago until this case is settled. I don't see any harm in telling you there was another homicide here recently," Todd said. "Just a little while before you came. Could be it was connected somehow to your uncle's death. Botetourt County doesn't exactly seem like a likely place for some kind of mass murderer to strike, but then you never know, do you? It happens in small towns now and then. Just watch your step."

Bates-Brennerman relaxed visibly. He ran his hand over his youthful-looking face and wiped it down the side of his jeans. "Yes, sir, I will. Morning, ma'am. Sir." He stood almost at attention for a clock's tick, then turned sharply and headed for the door.

When he was gone, Todd shut the door to the interrogation room. "I had an awful urge to shout, *dismissed!*" He laughed and dropped into one of the uncomfortable straight chairs surrounding the table.

"Cool cookie," Robinson said, sitting down across from Todd. She flipped off her high heels and massaged her toes. "I was pretty sure we wouldn't be able to break him by accusing him of D'Amato's murder."

"You think he bought it? You think he believes we don't suspect him?"

"Hard to say. He did seem relieved that we had another theory. Mass murderer! My God, man, was that the best you could do?" Robinson grinned amiably. Her crooked teeth, instead of detracting from her good looks, gave her face character. Her gray eyes sparkled as she spoke.

"For all his cool, he does give a signal when he tells a lie. Did you catch the eyebrow?"

"I didn't see anything. They said in the home office you were known for seeing clues nobody else could see." Her dark and graying hair fell across her forehead as she bent over to rummage through the leather briefcase at her feet.

Todd shrugged and smiled. "Guess I used to be pretty good at getting the truth out of people. Haven't had much practice lately. The worst we usually get is a Saturday night drunk-and-disorderly. Sometimes I miss the challenge."

"Well, brother, you've got something worse now." Billie Robinson located the folder she sought and pitched it across the table. "You can read this later," she said in a voice that hinted of hoarseness, "but I can tell you the important things now. The FBI took an interest in Brennerman after he got out of the Marines. I was in on it from the beginning. Now I guess you could call this case my baby. Found out he was involved in some small arms dealings with the Cubans. We think he started before he got his discharge."

Todd said, "What about that other stuff you were talkin' about on the phone last night?"

"Well, when he came out of the service, he hired on with the Mafia as a hit man for a while. We watched him, but he was good. Damned good! Never could get enough on him to arrest him, even though we knew what he was doing. Then about a year or so ago, he just disappeared. I thought some mark probably got him first. That he was dead. But — here he is, big as life. And it looks like he's involved in something else now. Wish I knew what. It could be Mafia connected." She stretched her legs out under the table and stuffed her hands deep into the pockets of her skirt.

"Isn't there something we can do besides just watch him?" Todd asked impatiently.

"Hungry for a little action, huh? No. I think that's the best we can do for the moment. Maybe he'll lead us to whatever he's involved in. We have him under twenty-four hour surveillance. If he breathes, the FBI will know it. Count on it." Billie Robinson stood up and stepped into her shoes. Then she stuck out her hand.

Returning the hearty handshake, Todd said, "Be a pleasure working with you. Never worked with a woman FBI agent before."

"Never worked with a man who could read facial tics either," Billie said gruffly. "Doesn't bother me."

It was nearly midnight before Billie settled down on the sofa of her Washington, D.C. apartment with a nightcap and her *personal* file on the Brennerman case. She propped her aching feet on the coffee table and pulled the terry cloth robe close up around her neck, then rubbed her temples hard with her thumbs as if she could shut off the thoughts gathering in her brain. It had been a long day with lots of memories. Old, painful memories that she had worked hard to keep at bay.

She had not told Todd the whole truth about the case. There were details he would never know. Didn't need to know. Details that clamored within her heart and soul on this night.

The file had fallen open as if it had a mind of its own to the date September 12, 1985. The name Mary Scott jumped out at her. Billie had teasingly called her Mary, Queen of Scots. She had been regal, commanding great respect in a department staffed mostly by men. It had seemed natural for Mary to be her mentor when she had first come to the FBI. And Mary had been her lover. Her very secret lover.

The Brennerman case had been Mary's to begin with. Billie had only helped with some of the paperwork, the kind of background information that was part of any case. What she knew was that the Chicago *cosa nostra* had connections inside the government: politicians who gave them information that helped them stay an arm's length away from the FBI and the drug enforcement boys. Mary had been on the verge of discovering the name of one of their contacts, someone very high in the government, when the phone call had come one night.

"Billie," the voice said, "I hate to be the bearer of bad news, but Mary . . . Mary was shot this afternoon in Chicago, working on that Brennerman thing. I'm sorry, Billie, but she's dead." There was a long silence.

"Billie, are you there?" the voice went on.

"I'm here," she managed. "What happened?"

"We're not sure. You know she was working on that Mafia connection in the government. It looks like she may have gotten too close. Our contacts say it's probable that Marvin Brennerman killed her. We may never be sure exactly what happened, Billie. She was working undercover."

Undercover. Shot. Dead. Part of the FBI game. Just to be expected. Take it in stride, Billie. Take over Mary's case, Billie. Oh, Billie, don't you weep, don't you moan.

But she had wept. And she had moaned. And she had made up her mind to get Brennerman if it took the last ounce of strength she possessed.

Then he had disappeared. And now here he was again.

Her hand trembled slightly as she reached for the cigarette pack on the coffee table. "I'll get him, Mary. I'll get him for you." And the smoke burned her eyes and she cried for the first time in months.

Chapter Nine

1

The boat Redman had promised was delivered to Wash's dock three days later. Jessie had told Wash the story about the money she was offered and the veiled threat Redman made against Meredith. They agreed that under any circumstances, whether or not Redman had anything to do with her father's death, it was best to cooperate. Wash would run his own boat until he could find another helper.

Then Jessie headed for the nearest pay phone to call Mel Todd.

"If you want," Todd said when she told him what had transpired, "I can arrest Redman right now, but from what you say, I'd only have to turn him loose. A threat gives me no legal reason to take action. Without some hard evidence, I can't hold him."

"I know that, Sheriff. I just wanted to let you know what was going on, you know, in case something happens to me."

"And you think your father was working for these people?"

"I don't know that for sure, but I do know that the fella who chased us that night thought we had something worth a lot of money. He said about a quarter of a million dollars. I guess he could have believed we had drugs worth that much. That's the only thing I can think of."

"Thirty-five or forty pounds of coke would be worth that much on the street. Maybe more, depending on how much coke is available. I don't like this, Jessie, it's too dangerous. I wish you'd just come on home and let me assign a special deputy to watch you."

"We've been through this, Sheriff. I'm going to learn what I can and then I'll get back to you. And listen, don't send anybody over here trying to find me."

He was about to tell her about the things he was

having Sybil send her, but she hung up before he could say any more.

2

When Walter Anamus came into Coxson's office that afternoon he was grinning from ear to ear. He sported a pair of purple wraparound sunglasses. His step was more a heel-to-toe rolling motion than a real walk as if he might break into a dance routine any minute.

"Coxson, old man!" he said, and dropped into a chair without an invitation. "I've got something for you. Something you want. Real bad."

Coxson looked at him steadily. Animal's gregariousness came as a surprise. "If you've got the girl, I want her."

"I've got her all right. All I have to do is pick her up. But we've got some talking to do first." Anamus pushed the sunglasses up so they rested in his dark hair.

Coxson swallowed hard. Seeing Animal like this was eerie. Up until now he had hardly done more than grunt a hello. Fear hit him solid in the gut and made his mouth as dry as parchment paper.

Animal leaned forward over Coxson's desk with an expression of undisguised contempt. "We're going to make a deal, *Mister* Coxson. And I won't take any shit about it either. You understand that?"

Coxson tried to laugh but it turned out to be a snort. "I don't make deals, *Mister* Anamus," he finally choked out. He knew his fear was showing but he couldn't stop it.

140

"You'll deal this time."

"You're making a big mistake, Anamus. What makes you think this *girl* is so important to me anyway?"

"Oh, I know it's not the girl herself. You could've just had me blow her brains out and be done with it. That's what I usually do for you, isn't it? Waste somebody who's givin' you a little trouble? But not this time. Not this time." Anamus jumped up from the chair and paced back and forth in front of Coxson's desk.

"You've lost your mind, Animal," Coxson said, not aware that he had called him by his nickname. "I could have you taken out of here on a spit."

"By who? All those little pissant soldiers out there? Didn't think I knew about that, did you?" He gave a high laugh that was mostly impatience.

"All I have to do is press a button and men will come —"

"Oh yes." Animal showed his large white teeth fully as he laughed. "They would all come on the double. But you'd be dead by then, wouldn't you? Then you'd never get into the White House." He sat down suddenly.

Coxson gawked at him. "Is that a goddamned threat? What do you mean, the White House?"

Animal ignored the questions as if the answers were too obvious. "And you wouldn't have that little lady who knows your secrets. The one who can blow your cocaine dealing in the Chesapeake Bay right out of the water, so to speak." He whooped at his own wit.

Coxson's thoughts were scrambled. How in bloody hell could Animal know so much? Of course he knew about the cocaine. He'd sent him to New Jersey to set up a new drop but nobody off the island knew about the soldiers. And *nobody* knew about the rest of the plan. Unless Miss Beck had . . .

The horror of the situation began to fully penetrate. This paranoid monster, this psychopathic giant knew everything! Coxson's breath came in large wheezes as fury flooded through him. "That whoring twit. What else did she tell you?"

"Twit? Nobody had to tell me anything. All I had to do was make a little trip to the library. Read up on some newspaper history. The rest was elementary, my dear Coxson." Animal was grinning like a comic book devil as he continued, "Colonel Ralph Harrington, formerly of the U.S. Marines," he began in rote fashion. "As of late, the President of the U.S. of fucking A. Sent your whole unit into the thick of things in Vietnam without a prayer in hell of getting out alive, didn't he? Only he came out a hero and you came out with a wheelchair, right? You lay right there, on the battlefield, didn't you, and watched your men blown to smithereens."

"You don't know what you're talking about." Coxson made a sound resembling a giggle.

"Don't I now? It's a matter of public record, Coxson. All the names are there. Including yours. *Captain* Coxson. Don't try to shit me. You're gonna try to take him out, aren't you? Pay him back in spades. You're gonna try to take over the fucking White House." Anamus began bouncing his legs up and down on the tips of his toes, making his thighs jiggle.

"You're a crazy man. Who would try to do such an idiotic thing?"

"A man who wants revenge, that's who. Like you do. You're the crazy man, Coxson, but you might just pull it off. I must admit the soldiers surprised me," Animal went on. "I thought you were just a happy little cocaine runner, until you were stupid enough to fly me out of here in a helicopter. Got a little careless in the heat of the moment, didn't you? Did you think I'd believe all those barracks were dog kennels?"

"They're not —" Coxson began lamely.

"Just to make sure, I did a little checking with an arms dealer I know. You *are* aware that I know some pretty despicable characters, aren't you? Or do you think I'm a holy roller on my days off?" Anamus reared back in his chair and crossed his legs. He looked like a man who couldn't wait to drive the next nail into the coffin.

Coxson stared at him with disbelief. He tried to calm down and think reasonably.

"Oh my, Coxson, you do buy a lot of guns just to protect a little snow!"

"What do you want, Animal?" He knew the charade wouldn't play any further.

"Not much. Just half the dope action and most of everything else you've got. I like fine things. Big cars, houses, fast boats. I've had papers drawn up for you to sign, transferring half of everything over to me. You know what I mean, you crippled old fart."

Coxson ignored the vicious remark. "Why should I do that, even if what you say is true? What's to keep me from having you killed the minute you step out of this office?"

"Because I've pulled the simplest little scam you can imagine." Animal laughed out loud. "Right out of

143

a paperback novel. You see, there is a lawyer who is sitting on a fuckin' in-the-event-of-my-death letter. If he doesn't hear from me once each month, that letter goes straight to six east coast newspapers. It's got the whole story. Dope, your little army here, your plans for Harrington. Everything I need to destroy you and your little empire."

"You can't! I can't let you do this! It would ruin everything," Coxson sputtered. His hands were clamped around the wheels of his chair so tightly that his knuckles were bone-white. "No one would believe you anyway. They'll say you're just a brain-fried junkie, trying to blame your own guilt on somebody else."

"You underestimate me, my friend. I have plenty of proof that your army exists. How hard do you think it was to hire a plane to make photos? Then there are the receipts for the arms shipments and there's this uniform factory in Ohio that keeps really good records. Shall I go on?"

"There's no law against buying uniforms or guns."

"There *is* a law against trying to overthrow the government though. Or didn't you know about that one? All I really need to do is raise some serious questions. No doubt your cocaine dealings would come to light. That'll close up your action if nothing else does."

"I can't let you do that," Coxson said, unaware that saliva had started to dribble in a thin line down his chin. The veins in his temples were pounding visibly. "He threatened to court martial me if I didn't obey orders. Court martial *me*! While *he* kept his ass safe and sound at headquarters! Dammit! I'll get that fuckhead Harrington if it's the last thing I do!"

Silence.

"You'll see," he said lamely.

Anamus waited until the man's breathing had returned to normal. There was a new edge to his voice, a patronizing softness as he said, "All right. I understand the desire for revenge. It makes a certain amount of perverted sense. But you've let your hatred get in the way of good sense, Coxson. You've been too careless. This Andrews business just proves it. And if I can uncover your scheme, so can others. Step aside and let me take over the operation."

"Impossible."

"You're a lunatic."

"I know. And you have more *gall* than any man I know, but I won't turn things over to you. I have to do this myself."

"You'll do what I say if you know what's good for you."

"I won't let you take over. I can't. But I'll sign whatever agreement you want when you give the girl to me."

Anamus thought it over, then said, "I don't have any real desire to shut you down. I'll even try to help you as long as you give me what I want."

Anamus had him. Coxson knew it. Even if he was bluffing about the pictures and the letter, he still knew too much. The loud ticking of the clock on the mantel beneath FDR's picture counted off the seconds.

Animal stood up suddenly and, with the stride of a victor, walked over to face Roosevelt's picture. He

145

stared up into the famous mole-endowed face for a long moment. "Did you know, Coxson, that FDR's wife was a lesbian? Good old Eleanor had a female lover. At least, some people say that. I don't know it for sure, but I wouldn't be surprised if it's true, would you?"

Coxson shrugged.

"Makes you wonder, doesn't it? He may have been the most powerful man in modern history but his wife preferred a woman. Seems like the joke's on him, doesn't it?" Animal turned to face Coxson. "Ironic, isn't it, Coxson? Your hero let a woman get the best of him — and so did you!"

3

Taking a proper bath had become an obsession with Meredith. Between pulling a few weeds in the kitchen garden and tending to the tiny chicks that Sarah had given her, she had spent most of the last seventy-two hours turning one corner of the dining room into a bathroom of sorts. The floor had been waterproofed, a plastic partition hung and an old-time claw-foot tub sat in middle. She had found the chipped and filthy tub back in the woods covered with honeysuckle vines and had persuaded Wash and Jessie to help her drag it into the house so it could be cleaned. She had spent the last two days designing a drain out of a bucket and some old garden hose. She had finally made it all work by setting the old tub up on concrete blocks and running the hose out a hole in the wall into the yard. Water had to be heated on the kitchen stove and carried to the tub by the bucketful but that was a small matter for someone who hadn't had a decent bath in over a month. A quick rinse at Sarah's now and then just wasn't the same as a good long soak.

"An everloving paradise," she exclaimed as Jessie came through the door. She lay nude and soapy in the tub with the partition drawn back. "That's where you promised you'd take me, wasn't it? To paradise?"

It was now Friday, the twenty-fifth of May.

Jessie pulled a wad of money out of her jeans pocket and pitched it onto the old table Wash had bought at a yard sale as a house-warming gift.

"Have you been in there all day?" she asked Meredith with a bite in her voice.

"I'd stay here night and day for a week if I thought I could get by with it," Meredith said, sliding down in the tub so that every part of her was covered with water except her head. "This must be the second best thing in the world."

"I made good money on crabs today, but Jesus, when is that Redman guy going to get going? I haven't heard a thing from him since he delivered the boat and the new crab pots." Jessie banged her hand on the table. For the last two days, she had come home from work exhausted and irritable.

"Slide a chair over here by me and I'll give you a kiss. Or better yet, take your clothes off and get in with me and I'll give you something better than that," Meredith said, thrusting her full breasts up out of the water.

Jessie stiffened and sat down at the table. One by one she began to count the wadded bills.

"What the shit's the matter with you?" Meredith demanded.

147

Jessie looked at her with a scowl. "Meredith, do you have to have such a foul mouth?"

"Jessie, what the hell is happening? All of a sudden I can't reach you at all."

"Nothing's the matter. I've just been working hard. I put out two hundred crab pots this week and helped Wash move another hundred out into deeper water. I'm tired to the bone. And I want Redman to *do something!* So far we don't have an ounce of proof he's doing a blessed thing that's illegal." Jessie stood up and started for the dining room door.

"Where are you going?"

"I'd like to take a look at the garden and the chicks before it gets late. That is, *if* that's all right with you."

"Jessie, wait a minute. Don't go. You've been as grouchy as an old bear for two days. Just tell me why. If you didn't want me to spend so much time working on the bathtub, you could have said so. And if money is worrying you, I told you I could probably get some painting work down at the wharf."

"It's not the bathtub, Meredith. Don't be ridiculous. What do I care if you have a bathtub? And we agreed you shouldn't work. Somebody might recognize you."

"Then come here and tell me what *is* wrong. Jessie, this isn't fair. I mean, if something's wrong I have a right to know too. I'm one half of us, remember?"

"If something's wrong, why would you want to know? Can't you just leave well enough alone?"

"Because we're fighting, that's why! And I get scared when we fight. In my family, life was just one long series of fights! I want to fix things. So

148

everything will be all right again." Meredith's voice was tinged with hysteria.

"Meredith, just leave things alone, will you? You want to poke and pick at every little sore till you finally get it to bleed. Just leave it alone. Can't you do that?" Jessie wheeled on her boot heel and headed for the door again.

"Damn you! Damnyoudamnyoudamnyou!" Meredith bit down on the cold washcloth and told herself to shut up. The clatter of Jessie's feet on the steps echoed in her ears as she heard the sound of Wash's truck in the front yard.

"Evenin'," she heard Wash say. "Guess you thought you were rid of me for the day, huh?"

"Thought maybe so," she heard Jessie reply. They talked quietly for five minutes or so, and Meredith lay still in the bath water trying to hear, but she could only catch an occasional word.

Finally Wash's engine cranked with a shudder, then caught. Jessie's boots hit the porch moments later.

"Meredith?" Jessie called as she came through the front door. Her mood seemed lighter.

"I'm still in here."

"A letter came from Sybil. It's a big envelope actually. I put Wash's return address on the one I sent. It came to his house today. I told him I'd been looking for it, so he brought it over." Her hands were trembling with anticipation as she tore open the bulky-looking envelope.

"Bring a chair over here by the tub and read it to me."

Jessie slid the chair noisily over beside her. Several items fell with a clatter as she accidentally

149

dumped the contents of the envelope on the floor in her hurry. "What's all this?" Jessie wondered aloud, picking up the articles. "That's my dad's wallet." She glanced through it quickly. "Nothing in it but his driver's license."

"Read the letter."

Crossing an ankle over her leg and leaning back in the chair, Jessie carefully unfolded the lined notebook paper and began to read.

"Read it out loud, Jessie."

"Okay. 'Dear Jessie and Meredith, The sheriff brought these things of your father's for me to send to you when he heard I got your letter.'"

"What's there besides the wallet?" Meredith interrupted.

"Just a key and a piece of paper."

"Funny looking key. Read some more."

"It says she was glad to hear that both of us are all right and that the sheriff has let your family know you're safe."

"Shit a brick," Meredith swore. "I'd just as soon they didn't know where I am."

"She doesn't say he told them where you are."

"Old busybody probably did. What else?"

"Just that they found some man dead up in Queen's Creek but they don't know who he is or who killed him."

"Nothing about what they know about your dad's death?"

"No. Nothing. That's kinda funny, don't you think?"

"Probably just means they don't know anything else. Do you have any idea what the key goes to?"

"I can't remember ever seeing it before. Let's see

what's on the paper." She unfolded the small bit of cardboard that had been neatly bent in half. "Says 201. It's a printed card. Something's been torn off the top. Do you suppose it has anything to do with the key?"

"I don't have any idea," Meredith said, then added with a dry chuckle, "the infamous mystery key. Sounds like something straight out of Nancy Drew, doesn't it?"

"Dad probably had a million dollars hidden away in some old trunk somewhere. Now all we have to do is find it!" Jessie laughed. She leaned over the side of the tub and slipped an arm around Meredith's shoulders. "I feel a lot better now, just hearing from Sybil. I'm sorry I've been such an ass lately."

"You're always an ass," Meredith said, giving her a forgiving look, "but what would I do without you?"

"Are you ever going to get out of that tub? Your skin's starting to wrinkle up and turn white. You look like a fish."

Meredith's hand shot up to grab Jessie's shirt collar. Before Jessie could recover her balance she was head first in the water.

"Let's be kissing fish, you old ass," Meredith giggled, splashing water on her face. "God, do you stink. You even smell like a fish."

"Well, why don't you give me a bath?" Jessie asked as she pulled her shirt over her head and kicked off her boots.

Meredith answered by rubbing soap generously over Jessie's breasts and kissing her deeply. It was late that night before they fell asleep, finally, in complete exhaustion.

At precisely 4:30 a.m., Jessie awoke covered with sweat. Her heart was trying to escape from her chest. As she propped herself up on one elbow and peered into the darkness, a strange vibration swept through her body, as if she were a human tuning fork. She felt like someone was watching her. Maybe someone was in the room. She looked at Meredith but she was only a vague shape wrapped in a sheet on the other side of the bed. Meredith's breathing was slow and regular. Even peaceful. Moonlight set objects off in bold relief as Jessie looked from one corner of the room to the other. She could see clearly that no one was there, but the feeling of being watched remained.

She got up, rubbing her eyes with her fists, like a small child aroused from a deep sleep by a bad dream. She stood still in the darkness, listening for strange sounds, but heard only the lonely hoot of a distant owl. There was something frightening and otherworldly about the sound that seemed to draw her toward the open window.

Out over the trees the moon was giving way to dawn, the rosy glow of pink-orange setting the pine tops in black silhouette. In the distance, laughing gulls picked up their morning cries while the hoot owl laid his own cry down for the daylight hours. She felt cold.

You thought you knew people, she reflected. Sometimes you didn't. Sometimes you were wrong. But you *would* think you knew your own father. Living with him. Working beside him day in and day out. God knows, if you couldn't trust that . . .

She stretched and yawned. Time to go to work

anyway. She thought of Wash and wondered why she felt such trust of him, then dismissed the thought immediately. Better not to build the monsters before they get in your closet by themselves.

She went to the bed and kissed Meredith lightly. Meredith moaned a sleepy sigh and turned over. "See you this evening, love," Jessie whispered and went downstairs to find her clothes.

Over the marsh land, the gulls wheeled in easy circles, waiting for the crab boats to pull away from the shores and provide them their freeloading breakfast.

Chapter Ten

1

Jessie glanced up at the sky as she jumped out of the truck at Wash's dock. A single dark cloud overhead brought a gust of wind that set the new boat rocking. She didn't want the weather to deteriorate now. A long summer blow would bring messy complications she didn't need. Surely the time would come soon when Redman would send her out to pick up something besides crabs.

She stood still, listening. Nothing. Except the usual early morning animal sounds and the soft wind in the trees. She loaded her arms with crab pot bait from the back of the truck and moved toward the shiny boat that Redman had provided. It was smaller than Wash's boat, a thirty-footer with an outboard engine, but it was wide of beam and had a small cabin for stowing equipment.

Briefly, she wondered where Wash was. He was usually at the dock getting ready for the day's work when she arrived. Humming softly, she set the heavy wooden box of bunkers aside while she untied the bow line. She walked back toward the heavy rope holding the stern to the dock.

It was then that she spotted the long body of Walter Anamus slouched on the boat's floor, next to the engine. He was dressed completely in black. His deep set eyes glittered wildly and his face was cut with a smart alecky grin.

"Mornin'," he said cheerfully, moving to gain his feet. "Sleep well?"

"Probably better than you if you slept in the boat," she said. The look on his face sent a stab of icy fear through her stomach. She tried to sound unflustered. "Where's Redman?"

"He sent me with a message."

"Fascinating," Jessie said with false bravado. "What is it?" She picked up the bait box and lifted it onto the deck. She had not expected this turn of events.

"Don't bother with that stinking shit today. You won't be needing it."

Jessie stood for a moment, breathing deeply,

evenly. Then she lifted the box back onto the dock and stepped onto the boat. "Am I going after the high-paying stuff today?"

"We're both going. I'm going to show you where it is."

"Is that necessary? All you have to do is give me the compass coordinates. I can find it myself."

"Yeah, it's necessary. You just get this boat going. I'll tell you where to go." To Jessie's astonishment, he pulled a gun out of his back pocket.

She frowned. "I'm not going anywhere with you. I work for Redman."

"Yeah? Well, Redman's not here and I didn't know I'd given you a choice."

Just then another man, a small man with tightly curled hair, came prancing out of the woods behind them. Jessie knew she'd seen him before. And she knew she was in serious trouble.

2

Wash Jenkins had been born with a veil over his face. His grandmother had told him when he was a little boy that he was very special because he would be able to tell what was going to happen in the future. Sarah had told him all it meant was that his mother's placenta was still wrapped around his head when he was born. He liked his grandmother's explanation about being special better, and besides, it was true that sometimes he seemed to know what was going to happen before it happened.

Fairly often he would have a feeling, some vague hunch that something was coming in the future —

and it did. Once in a rare while it was more than that. When it was more, he called it *seeing things,* and when he saw things, it was like watching a Technicolor movie that had actors and a plot. Seeing things was really different from having a hunch. It gave him a mind-splitting, skull-cracking headache.

Around four-thirty in the morning on that same Saturday that Jessie had been having insomnia, he awoke with a feeling that it was movie time. It started with a small calm voice that rattled and echoed around in his head: *Something's wrong with Jessie with Jessie with Jessie.*

He jumped out of bed as though he had been jerked up by a spring. His cotton pajamas were cold with a drenching sweat and in his head was a dull insistent throb.

"Washington?" Sarah always woke up when he left their bed. "It's not time to get up, is it?" She gathered the sheet and faded bedspread up around her neck. The morning air had a bone-chilling bite in it.

"Not yet," Wash answered. He pulled on his rubber boots and jeans over his pajama bottoms and stripped off the wet top. Sweat trickled down his thin rib cage.

"Are you sick?" Sarah reached over and turned on the table lamp beside the bed. The light cast shadows across Wash's dark face. "You don't look so good."

"Just a little headache I think. I'm going to the kitchen to get some aspirin. Go on back to sleep." He wiped at his chest with his pajama top and pulled a T-shirt over his head. He stumbled slightly as he moved toward the doorway.

In the kitchen he lit the gas stove, filled the

157

coffee pot. Within moments the smell of perking coffee permeated the air. Usually the aroma of coffee gave him a warm feeling, but now it made him a little sick to his stomach.

He sat down at the oilcloth-covered table to wait for the coffee. The faucet dripped steadily into the stainless steel sink. Without warning the tattoo of the throbbing in his head began to match the drip of the water.

Tall man. Tall man. Tall man. The phrase caromed inside his skull, increasing the head pain with every word. Wash rubbed his temples hard and leaned forward over the table on his elbows.

Tall man tall man tallman tallman tallman.

When it hit him, he thought it might take his head completely off his neck. His body snapped back in the chair as if something of great force had struck it violently and sucked the breath out. Then the vision came. All at once. Colors first, then forms.

Pale blue. The walls of a room. There was a room with two straight chairs and a small table. The ceiling was high. One window. Orange. Somehow he knew it faced east. The sunrise, of course. By looking out the window he could see the orangy tinge to the sky with dark pine trees in front.

Wash's thin frame began to shake and tremble as though some electrical current were passing through it. A low gagging noise passed from his lips. He tried consciously to push away the premonition, to not see the vision, but it was too late. It had started.

His mind skipped a beat. Black. A man in a black shirt. The tall man. Big muscular man, reaching for the woman's arm. Holding her tight. He could see it plainly.

158

"Who are you? What do you want?" the woman whispered. It was Jessie. Wash could see her dark hair, her face that was twisted into a grotesque mask of fear and surprise. The man said nothing.

The woman tried hard to pull away, but the man hit her across the face with something in his hand. Technicolor blood ran from her nose, across her lips and into her mouth. Red, bright blood. Wash could taste the blood thick on his tongue. He tried to wipe it away with the back of his hand but the taste remained.

"I can't breathe, please. I can't breathe! Stop! Stop!" Wash begged softly as he held his head tightly between his hands and rocked back and forth, squirming with the pain.

The smell of boiling-over coffee prickled in his nose. Another spasm hit him. He kicked one leg out straight, sending a cane-backed kitchen chair flying along the floor. He heard the sputter of coffee boiling over into the gas flame. He fought desperately against the vision, trying with all his will to hold it off. To stop the pain. Weakly he called, "Sarah? Come here, Sarah."

"Wash!" she yelled from the doorway. The noise of the chair falling had awakened her. She ran swiftly across the block-tiled floor and cradled him in her arms, rocking him back and forth like a mother with an injured child. "Wash, Wash, what is it, my darling?"

He slumped against her, resting nearly his full weight on her. He buried his head in the softness of her stomach and left a trail of blood from his mouth across her nightgown.

Sarah stared at the bright red line. "God, what

159

have you done to yourself, Wash? You've had a seizure and bit your tongue! You're bleeding!"

"Jessie," he muttered. "Save Jessie. The dock. He has her. The tall man. Get Mer —" His eyes gazed up at her briefly, unseeing. Then he collapsed forward over the table, spilling salt and pepper everywhere just as the sun blazed up over the horizon.

3

Jessie lay flat on the cool boards of the boat's floor, spread-eagled. Blood trickled in a thin rivulet from her nose, down her chin, and onto the collar of her shirt where it bloomed, flower-like. The small compartment of her mind that was still functioning could feel all of her muscles and tendons pulling tight, but there was no pain. The blow the tall man had delivered to her face had come as a complete surprise.

She tried to gather her power before it deserted her completely, before it ceased to be. She focused all her strength on staying aware and awake.

Her body was becoming a battlefield, with spirits fighting over her consciousness. Her mind seemed to split in two, one part desperately seeking oblivion, while the other dragged her upward toward the light.

"I'll help you," an urgent voice said.

"Wash?" she whispered. "Is it you, Wash?"

As if naming the force had suddenly given it strength, she felt powerful fingers reach deep into her brain. They wrapped themselves around her consciousness and pulled, almost viciously.

Jessie fought with all her might to maintain a

center. Rapidly she gained control of her mind. Then her body came to life again. As she stood weakly on her feet, she gagged and almost vomited from the wave of nausea that swept through her. Then, with a sudden, violent thrust, she found herself plummeted face down again. Something had grabbed the back of her neck and smashed her body forward.

With all the strength she had left, she rolled over on her back and lunged upward toward the body bending over her. She grabbed the man by his hair and clawed at his eyes. A slash of red appeared across his eyelid and down his cheek. Blood welled up in a fine line.

"You bitch!" he screamed as he covered his eyes with his hands.

Jessie fought to free herself. Her brain dazed and stunned, her body functioned reflexively, her hands groping wildly for a weapon, anything she could defend herself with.

The man circled her throat with his hands and began to squeeze slowly. He laughed. A demented cackle. "I'll teach you to fuck with Griffin Rather!"

Jessie tried to scream, but terrible sickening pain filled her lungs. She gasped for air and fought the impending darkness heralded by flashing colored lights behind her eyeballs.

From the dark mist came a sudden swell of sound. A bellowing that caused her body to vibrate in resonance. With dimmed eyes she watched as the man's head was wrenched backward. Then she felt the heavy pressure of his body lift away from her.

"You fucking ass!" Animal screamed at Rather. "I told you to leave her alone! You just love the smell of death, don't you? Can't you do anything right?"

He was holding the smaller man around the neck in a hammerlock, his head pulled back by his hair.

"She was gettin' away, Animal! I was just trying to stop her! Don't get excited, man. Getting mad at me won't accomplish anything."

"Yes, it will," Animal said. Anger oozed out of him like sap out of a tree. "By God, it will. It will get you out of my way permanently!"

Laughter rumbled in his chest as he calmly pitched the body of the smaller man over the side of the boat and into the creek. With easy concentration, he sighted down the cross hairs of his gun toward the bobbing body in the water and pulled the trigger.

A small curl of smoke rose from the barrel as he turned it toward Jessie. "Now get yourself together and get this boat underway."

She pulled herself up on one knee, then rose shakily to her feet. She was terrified, but something told her that if this giant of a man sensed how scared she really was, things would go worse for her. She shook her head to clear it.

"You'll have to run the damned boat yourself," she said. "Thanks to you and your dead friend, I can barely see two feet in front of me."

A torrent of angry words spewed from Animal: "You fucking stupid cunt! You do what I tell you to do! If it were up to me I'd just put a bullet between your eyes and be done with you! The only reason you aren't dead now is that Coxson wants to question you himself! Now move, dammit!"

Jessie turned away from him, pretending dizziness, weaving and swaying as if she might faint. Then she crumpled to the dew-damp floor of the boat. She needed a few seconds to think. Who was Coxson?

162

Animal was on her in a flash. Cramming the gun in his back pocket, he lifted her easily by the front of her shirt until her feet were in the air. With his free hand he slammed her hard across the face. Then he let go. She went down like a sack of rags.

Jessie felt her eye start to swell. She sent her tongue around inside her mouth in search of broken teeth, then struggled painfully to her knees. In scant seconds, she considered her options. Hand-to-hand combat with this giant? He was many times stronger than she. What chance would she have in such an uneven contest? He would tear her to pieces. And there was nothing to use as a weapon. Anything she might use was neatly stowed away in the cabin. And that left her brains. If she had a chance at all, she would have to outsmart him.

"Now get up here, bitch, and run this boat. It doesn't pay to cross me. You do what I say and I won't hurt you any more."

Something was wrong here. Why did he not just tie her up and get on with taking her wherever he intended? There was extra rope for the crab pots on the deck. Could it be possible . . . She got to her feet and moved forward to start the engine.

4

Sarah ran as fast as her chunky body would carry her through the woods to find Meredith. Sweat streamed down her face and her heavy bosom heaved as she beat on the front door of the house. "Meredith! Meredith! Come here quick! Let me in!"

"What's the matter, Sarah? Has something

163

happened to Wash?" Meredith pulled a sweatshirt over her jeans as she opened the door.

"Not Wash. It's Jessie. Wash had a premonition. Someone has kidnapped Jessie! I'm sure of it. Wash is never wrong."

For a second, Meredith stood frozen. "She's not —"

"Dead? I don't think so, but we've got to get to the dock right now. Hurry. I've got Wash's squirrel gun. You take it and go on."

Meredith hit the front door so hard the screen door broke and she ran barefoot ahead of Sarah through the woods.

5

"Feeling better?" Animal asked Jessie as the boat cut easily through the waters of the Chesapeake Bay. The sun gleamed off the revolver that rested in his lap as he lounged comfortably behind her on the boat's wide gunwale.

Jessie eased back on the throttle, slowing their forward movement slightly. "What the hell do you care?" she snapped back. The pain in her head was causing anger to rapidly replace fear.

"Oh, I do care. Very much. You're worth a great deal to me."

Glancing quickly back over her shoulder at him, Jessie could see that his eyes were not the same as they had been moments before. The crazed look was still there, but the anger was gone. She asked, "Do you really expect me to believe that, after you busted my face? My nose feels broken."

"I coulda done a lot more. Probably would have if you hadn't been such a lady." Animal threw his head back and laughed.

"What do you —" she began, and felt him move up behind her.

"Don't mindfuck with me," he said, ringing the back of her neck easily with his long fingers. "I know who you are. I've been watching you for days. That whole thing with Redman was just a ruse so I could be absolutely sure you were the right one."

"The right one? You think I've got something? Is it drugs you think I've got? 'Cause I don't have a damned thing."

"Listen, *Miss* Andrews, I even saw you parading around the house in your birthday suit. Don't put on any acts for me. I know all about you."

"You intend to rape me? Is that it?"

"You're not bad naked, but definitely not my type. No boobs. But I must admit that girlfriend of yours, she thinks you're tough shit." Then he laughed like a madman.

Jessie flushed as she gripped the boat's controls with a death grip. "You asshole," she said quietly. "What do you want with me?"

"I've read about lesbians. Butches. Femmes. Dykes. Isn't that what you call 'em? And I don't get it. Can't see for the life of me what you want with each other. Some people say all you need is a good lay." He laughed again, tightening his fingers on her neck.

"You'll have to kill me first." A muscle jumped in her jaw.

"Men, I understand." He went on as if she hadn't spoken. "Men have power. Penis power. Pain power.

165

Money power. I can see how two men could get it up for each other, but women? Women are useless, helpless, pieces of meat. How could a woman possibly prefer another woman to a man?"

"You got it all figured out, haven't you?" Jessie said contemptuously. "You don't know from apeshit! I asked you what you want with me. I told you I'd bring the drugs in for you. What the hell is this all about?"

Instead of answering, Anamus looked at her thoughtfully, as if seeing her for the first time. He loosened his grip on her neck and said nothing more until they reached the mouth of Stutt's Creek and entered the bay. "Take a southeast heading," he said. "It's time you met the boss."

"What boss? I don't know why you can't tell me what's going on. You've got a gun on me. I'm not going anywhere. It's for damned sure I can't walk on water."

Anamus narrowed his eyes, then he laughed quietly. "It would be a hell of a note if you really don't know anything. All this goddamned trouble for nothing. What a laugh on Coxson!"

"Listen, mister —"

"The name's Anamus. Walter Anamus. I don't suppose it matters what you know now. Coxson's going to kill you anyway. So I'll tell you everything. You might even get a kick out of it before you die."

And he did.

6

Meredith reached the dock well before Sarah. "Jessie!" she hollered out across the water. "Jessie?"

No answer.

The only boat in sight was Wash's well-worn deadrise. It was similar to the one Meredith's father had owned. She looked it over to see if anything was amiss. Everything seemed in place. Then she ran back to where Redman's new boat had been tied. Nothing looked wrong there.

She tried to feel relieved. Surely Wash's premonition had been wrong. Jessie had just gone out for a usual day of crabbing.

She turned back toward the path. She would tell Sarah everything was all right. But her eyes fell on the abandoned box of crab bait. Then she heard the sound. From under the dock. A low gagging, coughing noise that made yellow bile jump up into her throat.

Meredith was waist deep in the cool water when Sarah arrived. "There's somebody under here," she said. "Maybe it's Jessie."

She gulped a deep breath and turned her head down under the murky water, pushing her body cleanly underneath the boards of the dock. Seconds that seemed like minutes passed before her hand touched cold skin, then hair. The hair felt wiry as she locked her fingers in it. Swiftly she pulled the body to her, then thrust her feet against the muddy bottom, driving them both from under the dock toward the light.

"Who is it?" Sarah asked as she reached for the body Meredith shoved in her direction. "I never saw him before."

Together they pushed and pulled the man onto the dock. Sarah reached for the artery in his throat.

"Is he alive?" Meredith asked.

"Barely. I'll turn him on his stomach."

"Wait. Let me get a better look at him." Meredith lifted herself out of the water.

"Look here," Sarah said, pointing toward his chest, "somebody shot him."

"It's that man from the rest stop. The one who pulled a gun on Jessie and me a few weeks ago. She told Wash about him."

The man moaned and opened his eyes. Water poured from his mouth and nose.

"Animal?" he whispered.

"Who's Animal?" Meredith demanded.

"Take me with you, Animal. I have to —" His eyes closed.

Meredith shook him hard. "Don't you black out on me! Where's Jessie? Tell me, you jackass!"

"Animal? I have to go to the island with you. Take —"

"What island? Where's he taking her? You tell me! Tell me!" Meredith screamed at him as she realized that he was on the verge of passing out.

"The island that —"

Meredith shook him again, but he was unconscious.

"Shit!" Meredith muttered. "Sarah, you call the rescue squad and the police. Call Sheriff Todd at the courthouse."

"What you gonna do, child?" Sarah asked, her eyes growing large.

"I'm going after Jessie," she said, moving in the direction of Wash's boat. "I don't know which island they were headed toward, but there aren't that many in this part of the bay. I'll check them all."

7

"So you can see," Anamus said, "you are a very valuable piece of meat to me. You are the key I've waited for all my life. You're going to get everything I want for me."

"I don't believe any of it. My father would never agree to run drugs, no matter what they threatened him with," Jessie said.

"Believe what you want to."

"You're gonna rape me, aren't you? Isn't that what you really want? You one of those freaks who thinks there's something special about sex with a lesbian?"

"Rape? Shit no! I get all the sex I want. Women *love* me. I don't have to rape anybody. You think it's because of my pretty face?" he asked sarcastically.

Jessie said nothing.

"Or maybe they think I'm brilliant. I am, you know. I know how to get anything I want. That's been my life's work. To learn that."

While the man talked, Jessie had been trying to come up with a strategy. If she didn't think of something soon, it was a cinch she was a dead woman.

"Well, how about taking your brilliance back there and switching to the other gas tank. I was planning to fill both of them this morning before you came along. The tank we're running on is about empty."

He stared at the gas tanks.

"There's a lever between the two tanks. Just turn it so it points toward the other tank," Jessie instructed.

"No, you do it," he said. "I don't know shit about boats." His face flushed as he spoke.

"Just turn the lever! I have to run the boat! Unless you want to come up here and do it."

He stood still for a moment, then moved cautiously toward the stern. He touched the lever like a man might pick up a black widow spider. "This thing?" he asked.

Jessie glanced back at him. "That's it. Just turn it so it faces in the other direction."

She watched until he did it. When she turned her face away from him this time, a wide grin spread across her face. She had a plan that just might save her life.

Chapter Eleven

1

Meredith had searched several miles of the Chesapeake Bay to no avail by the time Agent Billie Robinson made it to Mel Todd's office that afternoon.

"It looks like somebody has kidnapped the Andrews girl. I've got a couple deputies out looking for her, but the Chesapeake Bay is a mighty big place," Todd said after their amiable greeting. He sat down at his desk. "But since kidnapping is a federal offense, I called you. And this may have something to do with the Brennerman case."

"It just might. You might as well look at this," Billie said, handing him a piece of paper as she brushed cold cigarette ashes from the cuff of her tailored Carolina-blue jacket. The suit looked expensive and fit her well-built body nicely. "You're not going to like it."

The paper Todd held was embossed by the Seal of the United States. He scanned the contents. Then he read it more carefully. Then he read it again. He couldn't believe his eyes.

INTERAGENCY MEMO   Telex: 4356992

From: Seth Mullins, U.S. Drug Enforcement
    Agency
To: Wilhelmina Robinson, Federal Bureau of
    Investigation
Date: May 27, 1988
Re: Operation Chessy

Billie — I'm glad you contacted the DEA. We've had our eye on a drug importation operation down there in the Chesapeake Bay area for several months. We knew that large shipments of cocaine were being brought in, but not through conventional methods, e.g. yachts or airplanes.

I guess I have to brag a little because we've finally gotten nearly all of the marinas and small airports sewed up where this stuff used to come in. Once in a while somebody gets brave enough to land a light plane in a cornfield or push a boat up into some cove, but for the most part that attracts too much attention from the locals and makes it too risky.

For a few months we had the cocaine thing down to a trickle, then all of a sudden, boom, large quantities hit the streets again and we couldn't figure out how it was getting in.

As it turns out, some mastermind got the bright idea to get certain local watermen to bring the stuff in on their boats, along with whatever they were catching. The big boys would leave the stuff in waterproof bags out in the bay in crab pots or sometimes just in the water, marked by some kind of buoy. Then the watermen would pick it up and take it home with them (or to some other designated place) where it would presumably be picked up later by persons unknown to us.

As you have probably already guessed by the above account, one of the watermen, Andy Andrews, finally came to us with the story. Apparently, he saw an article on the agency in the local newspaper. He said a man he didn't know had approached him about the drugs, threatening to kill his daughter if he didn't cooperate. We talked him into going undercover for us. Our boys were to be present at Andrews' house when the mastermind's man came for the pickup so that we could attempt to find out who was behind the operation.

Unfortunately, for us and for him, things got fouled up. What we think happened was that the guy came to get the stuff before

Andrews expected him, and Andrews refused to give up the goods because we weren't there. The pickup man got excited and offed him. When we arrived the next night (when we had arranged for our little surprise to happen), he was already dead so we ducked out.

Obviously, we made some mistakes. We should have had him watched, etc. etc. But we didn't. What can I say? We were there when he told us to be and had no reason to think anything would go awry. Hindsight is a wonderful thing.

Meanwhile we've been watching the seafood docks to no avail. This agency would appreciate being apprised of any additional information which may come your way. We can probably supply some manpower to help you out if you need it and can assure the agency that this kidnapping is somehow related to the drug operation. Like you, we never have enough people to do everything we need to.

Wilhelmina "Billie" Robinson had been chain-smoking, mostly out of boredom, while Todd read the memo from Mullins. "Well, what do you think?" She spoke with the disinterested tone of a college professor who already knew the answer to the question.

"I think the DEA boys should've come to me when Andrews was killed. Goddamn you all! You keep your stupid secrets from us little guys, but you never hesitate to use the hell out of us when it suits your purposes! If I'd known about this then, I'd have put Jessie under protective custody immediately and she'd

174

be safe right now. I'd have locked her up in the fucking jail if I had to!"

"Mel, Mel, Mel! Calm down! I admit you're partly right. We don't cooperate with local cops like we should, but it isn't going to do you or me any good for us to be pissed with each other. I promised I'd give you all the help I can, and I will. This whole business is important to me. For personal reasons," she added, then went on quickly, "I've been after Brennerman a long time and I believe he's involved in this. Would it help if I said I was sorry? Should I shed a few tears of shame?" She gave Todd a crooked grin. She thought he was okay — for a man. He seemed to be one of those rare ones who had sense enough to respect authority more than gender.

"All right, all right," Todd said, still grumpy. "I know you're right. It's just that right now I'm up a creek without a paddle. We don't have a notion in the world where to go next. Jessie Andrews could be anywhere. And that damned Tompkins girlfriend of hers has gone out trying to find her! Now I've got two of them missing!"

Billie smiled in sympathy and stood up. "Oh, things aren't that bad, Mel. We've still got Micky Bates. Sooner or later that guy is going to make a move. He's not going to sit still forever. I have a feeling he's going to lead us right where we want to go. Meanwhile we have to wait. Patiently. Okay?" she added.

Mel Todd nodded. It wasn't okay for him, but it would have to do.

"Oh, by the way," Todd said, standing up with her. "The woman who called me about the kidnapping says her husband wants to come talk to

175

me. I know this sounds crazy, but she said he has visions about what's going to happen. Clairvoyance, I think they call it. And he had a vision about this case. Thinks he knows something that might help." Then, feeling a little foolish he added, "Guess that would just be a waste of time though."

Robinson smiled. "Don't look so sheepish, Mel. You'd be surprised how often the Bureau uses psychics. We don't usually put it out for public consumption, but we've sunk a hell of a lot of money into research on ESP and such."

"You think I should talk to him then?"

"I can't see that we've got a lot to lose, can you?" Billie lit another cigarette off the butt of the one she had just smoked, and coughed loudly. "There ought to be a federal law against the manufacture of these damn weeds, but I do love 'em," she said.

2

Walter Anamus had been honest with Jessie. He didn't know shit about boats. Once or twice he'd been a guest on somebody's yacht, but mostly he preferred to do his traveling by air. He and Jessie had been skimming across the water for less than an hour when the engine sputtered, then died.

"Dammit!" he said as the boat drifted to a quiet stop. "Fucking foreign-made engines." He made a gesture with the gun toward the 115 horsepower Yamaha that hung over the stern and into the water. "You know anything about fixing 'em?"

"Yeah. A little bit," Jessie said and grinned.

Animal didn't grin back. "Then get your ass back

here and see what you can do with this piece of junk."

She looked at him squarely. "Give me one reason why I ought to."

Animal's eyes widened slightly; then he pointed the pistol in her direction. Jessie felt something hot pass her head. A warm push of air followed. Then the gun's boom fell on her ears, deafeningly loud.

"I'll kill you right now if I have to. You can believe I won't sit here and let the Coast Guard pick us up."

"Guess that's reason enough," she said dryly as the pungent smell of gunpowder filled her nose. She headed back toward the engine. She knew what was wrong with it. Little by little she had opened the choke on the control panel. It was royally flooded.

As she passed by his huge body, Animal grabbed her roughly by the shirt and flung her toward the engine. "Don't fuck with me," he said.

Jessie said nothing. She knelt on one knee, then flipped back the catches that held the engine cover in place and set it aside. Gasoline fumes filled the air. "Smells like a gas leak."

"Fix it then, and do it fast."

"I'll need a screwdriver."

"Then get one, goddamn it."

"Got a little one in my pocket that'll do the job."

"Get it, but move slow."

Jessie looked over her shoulder at him as she reached carefully into the pocket of her jeans and withdrew the pocket knife. She held it out in front of her. "See? Just a knife that has a screwdriver blade." Quickly she opened it and turned back to the engine.

Animal moved up behind her to watch, but by the

time he had taken the steps to get there, she had nicked the fuel line. Gasoline dripped steadily down the black tubing, making a puddle in the bottom of the boat.

"Damn," she said, "this line is leaking. I need some electrical tape."

"Where is it?"

"Up in the bow in that red toolbox."

"Stay where you are. I'll get it," Animal said and retrieved the metal box.

"Won't take a minute," Jessie told him as she wrapped the black plastic tape around the split in the line. "There. That ought to hold her." Then, for show, she adjusted a screw in the front of the engine. "You want to try her now?"

"You get up there and start the damn thing," he said, pushing her toward the controls. "And don't try anything cute." He licked his lips.

Jessie turned the key. The engine groaned but didn't catch. Then she tried again. And again. Nothing.

"Must not be getting enough power," she said. "Maybe the battery is weak."

"What do you do about that?" Animal asked uneasily.

"That's simple. Just connect the two posts of the battery. That'll double the power. Just take that long screwdriver in the box there and lay it across those two little silver things sticking up. You hold it while I crank the engine." Her eyes held his as she spoke, trying to see if he recognized the lie.

He stood statue-still for a moment, then bent down for the screwdriver. "You'd better not be trying to pull anything," he said, and laid the metal shaft of the tool directly across the battery terminals.

She heard one small cry of surprise as sparks showered the back of the boat. Then as the hot flames mushroomed, she dove head first over the side of the boat and into the cool waters of the bay.

3

Wash and Sarah were talking with Sheriff Todd around the long table in the interrogation room of the Sheriff's Department.

"I've sent deputies over to Quinn's Inlet to look for Jessie and Meredith. I'll tell you though, we don't have much to go on. If that fella *is* taking her to one of the nearby islands like you think, we can search them, but there are a lot of other islands in the bay."

Sarah Jenkins said, "We just want to help all we can. We're fond of Jessie, and Meredith too. They've become like family." She nodded to reassure Todd that she was telling the truth.

"What I need now is a description of what happened when Jessie was kidnapped. Griffin Rather, the man you pulled out of the water, has recovered enough to tell us his version, but you may be able to add something that will be important."

"Sir," Wash interrupted politely, "we talked this over on the drive up here an' we think there's somethin' maybe more important to talk about first."

"Sure." Todd stretched his long legs out under the table and laced his fingers together over his thick

179

leather gun belt, ready to listen. He wished Billie Robinson could have stayed on for this interview but she had gotten an urgent call that took her back to the capitol.

Sarah began. "Sheriff, do you remember that Mr. Andrews had a key in his pocket when his body was found? You had Ms. Ekstrand send it to Jessie. It's this key right here." She took it out of her dress pocket and put it on the table in front of Todd. "Wash found it in the house after the girls . . . were gone. Meredith left in such a hurry this morning, well, we thought we ought to go in and look around. Make sure everything was turned off and all."

"Yes, I wondered at the time what that key might be to. It wasn't a type I recognized. I thought it might have something to do with his boat. Do you know what it's for?" Todd asked.

"When Wash found that key and held it, he got some impressions about it that might be important."

Todd stiffened involuntarily. It wasn't that he didn't believe in parapsychological phenomena; he guessed strange things did happen. It was just that he couldn't quite get over the feeling that things that couldn't be seen and touched couldn't be completely trusted either. "So what happened?" Todd said, trying to keep his skepticism hidden.

"Lots of people don't believe in this kind of thing, Mr. Todd," Wash said, as if he had read Todd's conflict and understood it. "But if you'd just be willing to listen anyways, it could be some help."

Sarah spoke for him. "What happened was that Wash got this picture — kind of a mental image I guess you could say — of a bird. A big bird with something in its claws."

180

"What kind of bird was it?" Todd asked, looking at Wash for an answer.

"I couldn't say, at first," Wash told him. "Then Sarah got the notion that I should draw a picture of it and here's what it looked like." He took a piece of paper out of his shirt pocket and handed it over to Todd.

Todd studied the drawing for a moment, then said, "That's an easy one. It's the eagle on the Great Seal of the United States. It's on the back of every dollar bill you ever handled. See the arrows in this claw and the olive branch in the other?"

"Yes sir," Wash replied, nodding. "You got it faster than we did, but we finally figured out that's what it was."

Todd ran his fingers through his thick gray hair. He couldn't decide whether to take this seriously or not. "Could mean a lot of things," he finally said.

"That's what we thought," Sarah said. "It could mean that her daddy might have some money hidden somewhere."

"It could also mean that the key has something to do with some place where you'd see the seal," Todd added, getting into the spirit of the puzzle in spite of himself.

"We thought about a bank," Sarah said.

"Yes," Todd said, scratching his head, "it could be a bank. I guess this could be a safety deposit box key. Or it could be a post office box key." He reached in his pocket and pulled out a set of his own keys. "Mine doesn't look like this one though. It's more round, where this one is long and slender. I guess keys at different post offices could look different."

"It don't look like mine neither," Wash said,

pulling his key ring out of his back pocket. "'Fraid I ain't never had nothing worth putting in a bank box," he laughed, "so I don't know what they look like."

"Well, one thing I can do," Todd said, feeling a little embarrassed that he hadn't thought to check out the key before he sent it on to Jessie in the first place. "I can have one of my deputies check all the banks and post offices in this area to see if Andrews had a box of either kind. It'll take a little time to get that done, but we can sure do it. We might just turn up something. Meanwhile I want you to tell me everything you know that happened when Jessie was kidnapped. Right now, we don't have any kind of lead on where she might be."

4

After the Jenkinses had gone, Mel Todd sat at his desk in the Sheriff's Department looking over the file Billie Robinson had given him on Marvin Brennerman, alias Micky Bates.

Todd tossed the file on his desk. Bates' connection with D'Amato linked him somehow to the drug smuggling, but how? Bates could be running the drug operation himself, but his history suggested that was probably not the case. Always, even when he was peddling arms to the Cubans, he had worked for somebody else. He had even been that kind of soldier. The kind that took orders extremely well. Like Ollie North, he could follow orders to the letter, but there was nothing to suggest that he had any leadership

182

qualities of his own. The file said the Mafia had told him who to kill and he did it efficiently, but he was never given any responsibility beyond that. Todd wondered how he was able to get up in the morning without someone to tell him exactly what time to do it.

And that damned psychic and his key . . .

The telephone startled him out of his musing. "Todd here," he said brusquely.

"Hello, Todd. This is Billie Robinson." The voice was high with excitement. "Things may be coming down, son! Our friendly Micky Bates just pulled out of the marina in his Sea Ox. The man I've had watching him just radioed it in. I've called the Coast Guard and they're going to keep an eye on him, but not get too close. You want to get in on the action?"

"You bet your life I do. I know you think this is a one-horse county, but we do have a big Mako with twin one-fifties on it. I'll have Bates in sight in fifteen minutes." His elation at finally having something to move on showed in his voice.

"Mel, be careful. We may be up against something bigger than either one of us has thought of."

Todd ignored the caution. "Where are you?"

"I'm heading your way by helicopter. I just radioed the Maryland Marine Patrol and they're getting a couple of boats ready for me and some of our other agents. We'll have a chopper in the air looking for Brennerman too. And I called Mullins. He's sending some of his agents like he promised."

"Billie, don't you ever feel guilty about having all that power at your fingertips? My God, it's just one man in a pleasure boat!"

183

"I'm going to be sure we don't mess up this time," she chuckled. "Besides, you're just jealous. Maybe I'll give you a job when all this is over."

"Not on a bet, my friend. Not on a bet!"

"You say that, but you're the one who's been so impatient!"

"Don't let that fool you! I'm just looking to be a hero, so I can be sheriff again. Folks around here wouldn't re-elect a fella who had to depend on the FBI to take care of his business!"

Billie laughed. "Don't worry. If we get him — when we get him — I'll see that you get your share of the credit! But you're not fooling me, Todd. You've missed this kind of excitement."

"Maybe a little." But that was all he would admit to.

Mel Todd put the phone back into its cradle. He ran to the gun rack on the wall and pulled down a .30-.30 shotgun loaded with Number 2 shot. The gun would blow a hole in the side of a building. "Better safe than sorry," he muttered to himself.

"Bob," he said to the deputy on his way out the door, "I'm going to be out in the Mako. I'll give you a call on the ship-to-shore as soon as I get underway. You hold the fort, okay?"

"Sure, boss, not to worry. And hey, I just found that safety deposit box. Andrews had one at the Commonwealth Bank in Lone Point."

Todd nodded and put on his sunglasses. Things were fast coming together.

Chapter Twelve

1

From the beginning Archibald Coxson had determined to keep careful and complete records of every part of his scheme to take over the government of the United States of America. He wanted to be remembered for his brilliance and bravery, but he wanted to be sure that his biographers knew as well that it had not been easy, nor had things always worked as smoothly as he had planned. After calling Bates to return to the island that morning, he had made up his mind about what he had to do. He sat down at his computer to compose another piece of his history.

Things have not gone as well as I would have wished during the past two months. It is my fault for not paying closer attention to the men who were being hired to run the drug operation. I must believe that I would have spotted D'Amato and Rather for incompetent imbeciles had I not turned virtually all my attention to the recruiting and training of troops here on the island.

The recruitment has gone quite well and has caused me little problem. Fortunately, for my purposes, there are hundreds of young men who love the weapons of aggression so passionately that they will fight in any man's army. They love spilling blood so much that, if they are unable to literally kill and maim, they will do it symbolically in weekend war games, and with bullets filled with red paint. Lately, most of my recruits have come from such camps, for they are eager for real blood. These men have not cared about my ultimate plan. Most have not even asked who they will fight against. The patriotism of my day, my war, has become a joke and a thing of history.

To date, I have more than one thousand fully trained guerrilla soldiers located in small towns around Washington, waiting for my command to attack the White House. I had hoped for at least another thousand men before the initiative was begun but I fear that

I no longer have the liberty of waiting. Too many things have gone wrong and there is too much risk that the drug dealing part of the Chesapeake Project will be discovered by the authorities. I must begin the invasion of Washington almost immediately, as soon as things can be organized.

I wish my biographers to know that I have no hope that the invasion will be more than minimally successful at this point, but I do expect that my primary goal, the destruction of President Ralph Harrington, will be achieved. It would have been wonderful to hold him prisoner and punish him, even as I was held prisoner and tortured those long months after I was abandoned there in the jungle. But I must be satisfied with his death and will rest in peace myself, knowing that he has been repaid for what he did to me. I must be sure that it is my own hand that pulls the trigger of the gun that kills him. That will be the ultimate justice for me.

There is much to be done in the next few days. I must deal with Walter Anamus. He cannot be underestimated. He is a cunning, dangerous and vicious beast who will stop at nothing to get what he wants. I should never have trusted him, and I do not trust him now. No matter what he says, he will take over this entire operation if I do not stop him. Perhaps had he not served me so well in the past I would have done something about him long ago. Another error of judgment which I hope I will not have to pay for.

The Andrews girl can be disposed of immediately. I have no further need of her since I have decided to go ahead with the military part of my plan. Again, it may have been a mistake on my part to worry about her. Certainly some of the difficulties I now face could have been avoided had I just let her go in the first place.

Coxson sighed, stored what he had just written, and turned off the machine. He looked at his own reflection on the blank screen. The lines around his mouth and eyes had deepened and his eyes looked watery, like a long-time alcoholic's. He felt suddenly old and very tired. There had been too many mistakes. It was time for the final scene and, perhaps, the final curtain.

2

Todd's ship-to-shore radio crackled with the sound of an off-shore morning thunderstorm. He had both engines wide open. Salt spray soaked his uniform. Periodically, he wiped his face with a handkerchief to see better through his stinging eyes. He couldn't afford to miss spotting the Sea Ox.

Billie Robinson's voice suddenly cut through the static. "Mel, I think I've got you in sight about two or three miles ahead of me. Can you slow down a little bit and let us catch up?"

"Sure thing," Todd replied. "How'd you get out this far so fast? You in some kind of miracle boat?"

"Nothing to it, my friend. We had the Maryland

Patrol boats start out ahead of us. Then the helicopters dropped us down by ladder. It's all in who you know," Billie added, laughing. Her spirits were soaring.

"How many boats have you got?"

"About a dozen. The DEA kicked in some of their patrol boats. Mullins is leading that pack."

"I'm here," Mullins broke in from his radio. "I've got you in sight too. We've got four boats out here now and two more on the way."

Todd whistled his disbelief into the microphone. "I'm afraid to ask, but how many people are with you?"

"Not more than twenty-five or so. It's the best I could do on the spur of the moment."

"Jesus, Mary, and Joseph! Why didn't you call the President and have him send out the whole friggin' Navy?" Todd asked, amazed.

"I thought about it," Billie called back, her laughter acknowledging the fact that she did enjoy the power. "But I was afraid it would attract too much attention. Besides, those big old ships burn too much gas. Hold on, I'm getting a call from the copter. He's on another frequency."

Todd looked behind him. On the horizon he counted ten dots bobbing across the waves, the distance between them rapidly closing. He cut his throttles back a little as he searched the sky for the plane.

"Mel, listen, my man in the chopper says he's spotted a small island directly in Brennerman's path," Billie reported. "He's moving southeast on a compass heading of about one hundred and fifty degrees."

"That would be Diablo's Island," Todd said.

189

"Some eccentric millionaire bought it from the state a few years ago."

"Maybe we know now what made him a millionaire," Mullins responded. "Lots of money in drugs."

"Listen, Mel," Billie broke in again, "the pilot says he's spotted some kind of fire about five miles south of his location. A boat burning like Hades. Think I should divert him over that way?"

"If you think we can spare him. Jesus, I hope it's not Jessie Andrews."

"Wait," Billie called back, "he says there's another boat headed in that direction. Someone else must have spotted the fire. I'll keep him with us."

3

If the man the FBI had identified as Brennerman had not been so lost in thoughts of his own, he might have noticed the chopper that hovered in the distance over the bay. But he was. And he didn't.

The call from Coxson had come as no surprise. He had been expecting it and wanting it. He had been living as Coxson's good little boy in Pliney Point long enough to get restless. Passive surveillance of hayseed cops was not his idea of living. The appearance of the FBI broad had added a little spice for a few days, but she had been as stupid as the one they'd sent to Chicago to find him. He could have taken her out fifteen times before the old man had given him permission to actually do it.

He wanted to get back to his job in Chicago. Something was always happening there. He had told

190

the Don when he called him just the night before
that he didn't care how dangerous it was, he was sick
and tired of sitting on his thumb.

Zooming along now on the waters of the
Chesapeake, he looked forward to what lay ahead of
him. His mind was whirling. There were so *many*
ways to kill. And Don Carmona had told him to do it
any way that would make him happy. He felt, he
thought happily, like the proverbial kid in the candy
shop.

4

Coxson spent the rest of the morning at the
computer console, working up a map which showed
the precise location of all his soldiers surrounding the
Washington area. He had deployed them in small
towns, like Purcellville and Dale City in Virginia, and
Gaithersburg and Crofton in Maryland, where groups
of ten or twelve men could pose as construction
workers without attracting much attention. When the
map was completed, he began to make his plans for
the immediate future.

His eyes flashed wildly as he looked forward to
having Bates take care of Anamus. He had considered
doing it himself, and if it wasn't for his useless legs,
his gift from Harrington, he would do that. But he
could not risk the possibility that Anamus would
outsmart him somehow. No, it was a job best left to
a professional killer like Bates.

Meanwhile he would finally have the girl. When
he had done with her and Anamus, he would have
Bates begin contacting the men to have them form up

191

in platoons. Within a few days, by his calculations, they would be ready for the Washington invasion. He would lead the men himself from an outpost in Arlington. He wondered idly if the cherry trees would still be in bloom.

5

Meredith had been searching the bay for hours, straining her eyes for some sign of Jessie's boat. She had circled Blood Island, then Guinea Marsh with no luck. Only John Smith Island was left.

It was hopeless. She was sure it was hopeless. They had killed Jessie's father and now they would kill Jessie for reasons she would probably never be sure of. Life without Jessie was more than her mind could fathom. Tears started down her cheeks.

Don't think like that, Meredith. Don't do it! You have to think clearly. You have to believe in what you want. You have to have faith in the future.

"Yeah, okay, you're right," she said to the voice in her head. "I know that. I believe that. And I will believe that Jessie's all right. I do believe that Jessie's all right. If I imagine Jessie being okay, she will be."

It was then that she remembered that there was another island in this part of the Chesapeake. A smaller one called Diablo's Island lay a little southeast of John Smith.

She glanced at the gas gauge on Wash's boat. Not

much left. Five gallons at the most. Enough to check out one of the islands, but not both. Diablo's was smaller but a little farther. Would anyone sell gas there? Which one first?

She still had not made up her mind, when on the distant horizon, in the direction she knew Diablo lay, she saw shadows move. Heat rising off the water. Then a flash. Like a dozen sticks of dynamite had been set off at once.

6

In his beautifully furnished office on the first floor of his house, Archibald Coxson sat at the window in his wheelchair, looking out over his estate. The large bay window gave him a breathtaking view of the wide lawn, and beyond, the glistening waters of the Chesapeake Bay.

Micky Bates opened the door and came in, slightly out of breath. Miss Beck bustled in behind him, protesting his unauthorized entrance.

"It's all right, Miss Beck," Coxson said, waving her away. "Go on with your business. Welcome back, Micky."

Miss Beck was still fuming when she closed the door behind her.

Coxson wheeled himself behind the hand-carved teak desk and looked almost lovingly at Bates. "Being in the sun has done you good, Micky. You look very fit."

"I got here as quickly as I could, sir," Bates said in a serious tone. "You said it was urgent that we mobilize the troops right away?"

Bates felt a shudder of pleasure plow through his stomach as he thought of how easy it was going to be to murder this trusting man. It was all he could do not to let a broad smile take over his face.

"We can take care of that later. Right now, there's another job for you to do. One I just couldn't trust to anyone else. Walter Anamus is on his way to the island. I want you to kill him."

"Yes, sir. That's fine." Bates replied, allowing himself to smile over the unexpected bonus. "Anything special you have in mind?"

Briefly Coxson considered some kind of slow and painful death, then dismissed the idea as too risky. "Anamus is a dangerous man, Micky. Just kill him and do it quickly."

Bates turned happily toward the door to leave. There would be plenty of time later to take care of the cripple.

"Oh, and Micky," Coxson added, closing his eyes in indecision. Then he squared his shoulders and continued, "There's a young girl with him. You might as well kill her too. Just don't mess it up."

"I certainly won't do that, sir. You know you can count on me!"

7

Down at the dock, McSwain's rifle fire and scream for help were lost in the racket of the motorboat engines churning the water.

194

Mel Todd pushed himself over the side of his boat and onto the landing platform with one hard thrust of his legs. He felt splinters dig into his arms as he sprawled forward, nearly onto his face. He uttered a small groan as the wind left his chest, but he held onto his gun.

McSwain reflexively jerked his gun in Todd's direction. He fired rapidly as the sheriff rolled to his left and regained his footing. The bullets dug holes where his body had been moments before.

Todd heard the sound of feet hitting the dock behind him as he raised his gun in McSwain's direction and pulled the trigger.

Terror flashed in the soldier's eyes as his body was knocked viciously backward. Blood sprayed from his right shoulder, instantly soaking the pristine white uniform. He could not stifle a cry of pain and bewilderment as he staggered, then hit the ground hard.

"What in the name of God —" McSwain screamed as he tried in vain to swing his rifle toward Todd.

Todd braced his right hand with his left and took careful aim at McSwain's head. His mouth was drawn down in a thin, hard line as he started the slow squeeze of the trigger. Two agents streaked by him, running toward the wounded man.

"No! Don't kill him, Mel!" Billie Robinson yelled. "We might need him."

Then there were agents all over the dock and Todd felt Billie touch his arm. Still he stood frozen in a classic shooter's stance. I'd forgotten, he thought, what it's like to kill a person. How easy it can be. Cold sweat ran down his back and his hand trembled slightly.

"Mel," Billie said gently as she pulled his arm down to his side. "It's okay. We've got him now. You did a great job."

Slowly he relaxed and became aware of the agents who were struggling with the gate that blocked their way to the island. Some were trying to cut the bolt that held it closed. Others scaled the fence and dropped to the other side. Mel watched them move slowly up the hill, guns ready.

He shook his head to clear it and lowered the gun. "I almost killed him. Just for the fun of it."

"Not for the fun of it, Mel," Billie said. "To save your life — and ours. Put it behind you. We have work to do. I think this man you shot just might be willing to tell us what we're up against now."

The tiny radio in the jacket pocket of her nylon jumpsuit popped incoherently, startling Mel. Billie explained, "I sent Mullins and some of his agents to work their way along the perimeter of the island. The helicopter pilot spotted what looked like guard posts."

Calmly, she unzipped her sleeve pocket in search of a cigarette, then spoke into the radio. "Seth," she said to Mullins, "what do you see out there?"

"Billie, you wouldn't believe what I see. We've taken care of the guards. But there's some kind of barracks and what looks to be a parade ground with bleachers and everything. We're getting ready to move in slowly and see what we've got here."

"Move carefully," Billie cautioned. "Whatever it is, we can't afford to screw this up."

"Don't rub salt in my wounds, dear lady. This time we're going to get it right."

8

Jessie was flipped over in the water by a belch of white hot heat. Waves of near panic gripped her as she groped for something, anything to hold on to. Then her sight dimmed and her eardrums almost burst. Everything was blurred and the air was full of thick choking smoke and bright flashes. The sky was raining pieces of boat around her head.

Still she was groping, unable to tell up from down, when she heard it. *"Jessie!"* a voice screamed. *"Jessie!"*

For a second she thought it was Meredith's voice, but that was ridiculous. Therefore she had to be dead. Because no one could possibly know where she was. Just before the darkness became complete, one of her hands found something to hold on to and she looked up into the face of an angel who bore a striking resemblance to Meredith.

9

The soldier Coxson had stationed in the Communications Room was munching happily on a tuna and rye sandwich when he finally noticed some unusual movement on one of the monitors. He took a last swallow of his coffee and got up to take a closer look. At first he thought one of the dogs had gotten loose; then he realized that whatever was moving down near the barracks wasn't white.

"Oh, holy shit!" he uttered and pushed the

button that turned on a warning siren that flooded the air over the island.

All hell broke loose.

10

Astonished DEA agents watched as fifty or so young men dressed in black Nazi-style uniforms poured out of what turned out to be the barracks' dining room. None of them carried arms of any kind, but the white uniformed officers who followed all had handguns. In the frenzy that followed, the officers fired wildly at anything that moved, including the blackshirts. The agents, who all carried automatic weapons, returned the fire.

Billie Robinson had started up the ramp from the pier to the house with her agents and Mel Todd behind her when the siren went off. "Form a ring around the house!" she yelled over the din. "Mel, you come with me. You wanted to be included in this. We're going in."

Todd's guts gave a lurch as if he were on the down side of a ferris wheel. He moved slowly forward. Out of the corners of his eyes he could see the others fanning out.

The front door of the mansion seemed to explode and belch out white- and black-suited men, spraying bullets as they came.

Billie's agents, wired for action, opened return fire, their faces grim and their eyes blank, as if they were moving through some kind of rehearsal for damnation.

Todd's feet seemed frozen to the front yard. He fired wildly into the mound of bodies that accumulated on the front porch. It had been years since he had been in this kind of a fray. Too many years. He kept shooting and shooting until all his bullets were gone.

"Come on, Mel! God damn you, come on!" Billie Robinson screamed at the top of her lungs. She was already halfway up the front steps, machine gun in hand.

Todd pitched his service revolver to the ground and screwed up the courage to follow Billie. Shifting his shotgun from his left hand to his right, he hit the steps running.

11

Archibald Coxson was in a state of wild panic by the time Micky Bates got back to his office. He would have fled the house when he heard the siren, but his lack of mobility made him a sitting duck. He had watched the slaughter on the front steps from a window, moving away only when a stray bullet broke a windowpane. He could scarcely hear the gunshots over the noise of the siren and Miss Beck's hysterical screaming. He would have gladly slapped her senseless if he'd been close enough.

"Thank God you're here, Micky. We have to get out!"

"How would you propose that we do that? You think we can outrun them with me pushing a wheelchair?"

"Think of something! Think of something, Micky! There must be some way!"

"Oh, there is," Micky said calmly, "and I've already thought of it."

"I knew I could count on you," Coxson began, then, too late, realized what Bates meant. His face blanched chalky white before he covered it with his hands.

"Don't worry, sir," Bates said, almost sympathetically. "This would have happened anyway. The Chicago Mafia had already given me permission to kill you. Your operation was getting too big. They don't like for people to cut into their profits. Besides, what was it you used to like to say, Mr. Coxson? 'Old soldiers never die'?"

Coxson's wheelchair lurched backward, then fell over from the impact of the .44 slug that caught him just above the right eye.

Micky turned back toward the door with a demonic gleam in his eye and found himself looking into the muzzle of a Government Issue machine gun.

"My name is Billie Robinson," the woman in the water-stained jumpsuit told him. "Remember me? And I believe you've met my friend Mel Todd. That was an interesting speech about the Chicago Mafia, Mr. Bates. Or is it Mr. Brennerman? Perhaps you'd like to tell me more about it?"

12

A warm rush of emotion filled Meredith when she saw Wash and Sarah standing on the dock, waving.

Wash secured the boat and climbed on board. "Where's Jessie?" he asked, looking worried. "She all right?"

"I think so. She's in the cabin. I tried to keep her awake, but she might have gone back to sleep. She's got a pretty big bump on her head. Redman's boat exploded and knocked her unconscious for a few moments, just before I found her."

"Not good for her to sleep until we make sure she's okay. I'll get her up and walking."

Meredith jumped from the boat and embraced the stocky Sarah. "How'd you know when we'd get back?"

"Well," Sarah said, smiling broadly. "I could say Wash had a vision, but it ain't so. We decided to wait here for you, no matter how long it took. Even if it took all night. The Coast Guard's out there searching for you."

They looked toward the boat's cabin as they heard Jessie moan and yell out, "God, Wash, let me alone. My head hurts and I'm tired."

"What happened to the man who took her?" Sarah asked.

"I looked all around where I found Jessie but I didn't see him. The bay can take a body away pretty quickly."

"We better call the Coast Guard and tell them where to look," Sarah said.

Wash appeared at the cabin doorway with Jessie leaning on his thin body. "I told her she had the whole winter to rest. We have work to do before the crabbin' season ends."

Jessie grinned. "Now you know why I quit working for him. He works me too hard!"

"In that case, I'll just hire Meredith," Wash told her. "Seems like you ain't the only one around here whose daddy taught her how to run a crab boat!"

Epilogue

It was six o'clock on an October evening in Pliney Point. The sky was flooded with the dark, fast-moving clouds that sometimes precede a fall hurricane. It was a dreary evening for a celebration, but there was good reason to celebrate.

Jessie and Meredith had moved back into the Andrews house when crabbing season ended in Quinn's Inlet, leaving Wash and Sarah behind with lots of promises to visit often. With the money Jessie had earned working with Wash, they had begun to pay off the overdue mortgage payments and had even made a down payment on a new boat.

Wash had offered Jessie a job oystering with him during the winter, but she had declined with thanks, explaining that dredging for crabs in the cold months was what she liked best. The new dredges were to be delivered in about a week.

Meredith's sign-painting business was growing so rapidly that she hoped it would be thriving by spring. And she had said frankly that she was happy to get back to electricity and indoor plumbing. She was even learning to tolerate, if not enjoy, an occasional visit with her family.

"Hi, Billie! Sorry I'm late," Meredith exclaimed as she bustled into the warm kitchen. "Old man Simms wanted a grinning cat painted on that yacht he calls *The Cat's Meow*. It took longer than I thought it would. You started dinner yet?"

"Of course," Jessie said, making a face in her direction. "Did you think I'd wait all night for you?"

Meredith kissed the top of her head as she shucked off her coat and sat down at the kitchen table. "You'd *better* wait. I waited long enough for you!"

Billie Robinson smiled and poured Meredith a glass of the wine she had brought. "I hope you don't mind my inviting myself down like this. I wanted to see you again."

"Not at all." Meredith beamed. "We had so much fun when we came to Washington to visit you. Washington's such a big place and there's so much to do!"

"Yes, but I must admit I get lonely at times."

Billie stared into the burgundy liquid in her glass for a moment. "But hey, I'm making some new friends. Like the two of you." She raised her wine glass in a toast.

"It must have been awful for you to lose Mary. When I think about how close I came to losing Jessie —" Meredith's voice trailed off. "I'm sorry. Jessie says I never know when to keep my mouth shut."

"It's okay," Billie said. "Time has a way of taking care of things. Even the worst of things." She changed the subject. "Have you seen Mel Todd?"

"Poor man!" Meredith said. "I think he must have a crush on you, Billie. He found all kinds of excuses to drop by here when he found out we'd become friends with you."

"Don't think his wife would like that too much," Billie said. "He really misses the excitement of being a big city cop sometimes, no matter how much he denies it. And besides, I think it just fascinates him that the FBI would hire a woman."

"It fascinates me too," Jessie said. "He told us Micky Bates got a life sentence."

"Yes, thank God," Billie said. "I'd have done anything to see him behind bars. I know in my heart he shot Mary, and who knows how many other law enforcement agents. He's a vicious killer!"

"How in the world did you get into such a dangerous business?"

"Oh, it's a long story, Jessie. I'll tell you about it sometime. Right now I want to tell you some great news."

Billie dug around in the pockets of her designer

jeans. Then, brushing her dark hair from her face, she started in on her pocketbook. "I know it's here somewhere."

Jessie frowned and looked puzzled. "Don't tell me it's another mystery!" She remembered well her father's safety deposit box which had contained the cocaine he had intended to turn over to the DEA.

"Nope, no mystery. But look at this!" Billie produced a small rectangular piece of paper and spread it out on the table.

Jessie broke the awkward silence that followed. "Damn! That's a check for twenty-five thousand dollars!"

"And it's made out to you, Jessie!" Meredith said gleefully.

"Seth Mullins from the DEA asked me to give it to you. Part of it's the money they'd agreed to pay your father for working for them and part of it's a reward to the two of you for helping us all with this case. After all, Jessie, you put your life on the line to help solve it."

"I did that for my father — and for Meredith — not for money," Jessie said solemnly.

"That's right," Meredith said, trying hard not to let her mouth turn up at the corners. "And," she added, "we've already got so much — good friends like you, Billie, and Wash and Sarah. Jessie has her new boat — and last — but not least," she said with a dramatic sweep of her arm, "we've got each other. So I'm just sure that Jessie will want to give that check right back to the government!"

"Meredith," Jessie said gravely. "Do you know something?" Her face broke into a broad smile. "Sometimes you're so full of shit!"

A few of the publications of
THE NAIAD PRESS, INC.
P.O. Box 10543 ● Tallahassee, Florida 32302
Phone (904) 539-5965
Mail orders welcome. Please include 15% postage.

CHESAPEAKE PROJECT by Phyllis Horn. 304 pp. Jessie &
Meredith in perilous adventure.   ISBN 0-941483-58-4 $8.95

LIFESTYLES by Jackie Calhoun. 224 pp. Contemporary Lesbian
lives and loves.   ISBN 0-941483-57-6   8.95

VIRAGO by Karen Marie Christa Minns. 208 pp. Darsen has
chosen Ginny.   ISBN 0-941483-56-8   8.95

WILDERNESS TREK by Dorothy Tell. 192 pp. Six women on
vacation learning "new" skills.   ISBN 0-941483-60-6   8.95

MURDER BY THE BOOK by Pat Welch. 256 pp. A Helen
Black Mystery. First in a series.   ISBN 0-941483-59-2   8.95

BERRIGAN by Vicki P. McConnell. 176 pp. Youthful Lesbian–
romantic, idealistic Berrigan.   ISBN 0-941483-55-X   8.95

LESBIANS IN GERMANY by Lillian Faderman & B. Eriksson.
128 pp. Fiction, poetry, essays.   ISBN 0-941483-62-2   8.95

THE BEVERLY MALIBU by Katherine V. Forrest. 288 pp. A
Kate Delafield Mystery. 3rd in a series. ISBN 0-941483-47-9   16.95

THERE'S SOMETHING I'VE BEEN MEANING TO TELL
YOU Ed. by Loralee MacPike. 288 pp. Gay men and lesbians
coming out to their children.   ISBN 0-941483-44-4   9.95
                                         ISBN 0-941483-54-1   16.95

LIFTING BELLY by Gertrude Stein. Ed. by Rebecca Mark. 104
pp. Erotic poetry.   ISBN 0-941483-51-7   8.95
                                         ISBN 0-941483-53-3   14.95

ROSE PENSKI by Roz Perry. 192 pp. Adult lovers in a long-term
relationship.   ISBN 0-941483-37-1   8.95

AFTER THE FIRE by Jane Rule. 256 pp. Warm, human novel
by this incomparable author.   ISBN 0-941483-45-2   8.95

SUE SLATE, PRIVATE EYE by Lee Lynch. 176 pp. The gay
folk of Peacock Alley are *all* cats.   ISBN 0-941483-52-5   8.95

CHRIS by Randy Salem. 224 pp. Golden oldie. Handsome Chris
and her adventures.   ISBN 0-941483-42-8   8.95

THREE WOMEN by March Hastings. 232 pp. Golden oldie. A
triangle among wealthy sophisticates.   ISBN 0-941483-43-6   8.95

RICE AND BEANS by Valeria Taylor. 232 pp. Love and
romance on poverty row.   ISBN 0-941483-41-X   8.95

PLEASURES by Robbi Sommers. 204 pp. Unprecedented
eroticism.   ISBN 0-941483-49-5   8.95

EDGEWISE by Camarin Grae. 372 pp. Spellbinding
adventure.   ISBN 0-941483-19-3   9.95

FATAL REUNION by Claire McNab. 216 pp. 2nd Det. Inspec.
Carol Ashton mystery.   ISBN 0-941483-40-1   8.95

KEEP TO ME STRANGER by Sarah Aldridge. 372 pp. Romance
set in a department store dynasty.   ISBN 0-941483-38-X   9.95

HEARTSCAPE by Sue Gambill. 204 pp. American lesbian in
Portugal.   ISBN 0-941483-33-9   8.95

IN THE BLOOD by Lauren Wright Douglas. 252 pp. Lesbian
science fiction adventure fantasy   ISBN 0-941483-22-3   8.95

THE BEE'S KISS by Shirley Verel. 216 pp. Delicate, delicious
romance.   ISBN 0-941483-36-3   8.95

RAGING MOTHER MOUNTAIN by Pat Emmerson. 264 pp.
Furosa Firechild's adventures in Wonderland. ISBN 0-941483-35-5   8.95

IN EVERY PORT by Karin Kallmaker. 228 pp. Jessica's sexy,
adventuresome travels.   ISBN 0-941483-37-7   8.95

OF LOVE AND GLORY by Evelyn Kennedy. 192 pp. Exciting
WWII romance.   ISBN 0-941483-32-0   8.95

CLICKING STONES by Nancy Tyler Glenn. 288 pp. Love
transcending time.   ISBN 0-941483-31-2   8.95

SURVIVING SISTERS by Gail Pass. 252 pp. Powerful love
story.   ISBN 0-941483-16-9   8.95

SOUTH OF THE LINE by Catherine Ennis. 216 pp. Civil War
adventure.   ISBN 0-941483-29-0   8.95

WOMAN PLUS WOMAN by Dolores Klaich. 300 pp. Supurb
Lesbian overview.   ISBN 0-941483-28-2   9.95

SLOW DANCING AT MISS POLLY'S by Sheila Ortiz Taylor.
96 pp. Lesbian Poetry   ISBN 0-941483-30-4   7.95

DOUBLE DAUGHTER by Vicki P. McConnell. 216 pp. A Nyla
Wade Mystery, third in the series.   ISBN 0-941483-26-6   8.95

HEAVY GILT by Delores Klaich. 192 pp. Lesbian detective/
disappearing homophobes/upper class gay society.
                                        ISBN 0-941483-25-8   8.95

THE FINER GRAIN by Denise Ohio. 216 pp. Brilliant young
college lesbian novel.   ISBN 0-941483-11-8   8.95

THE AMAZON TRAIL by Lee Lynch. 216 pp. Life, travel & lore
of famous lesbian author.   ISBN 0-941483-27-4   8.95

HIGH CONTRAST by Jessie Lattimore. 264 pp. Women of the
Crystal Palace.   ISBN 0-941483-17-7   8.95

OCTOBER OBSESSION by Meredith More. Josie's rich, secret
Lesbian life.   ISBN 0-941483-18-5   8.95

LESBIAN CROSSROADS by Ruth Baetz. 276 pp. Contemporary
Lesbian lives. ISBN 0-941483-21-5   9.95

BEFORE STONEWALL: THE MAKING OF A GAY AND
LESBIAN COMMUNITY by Andrea Weiss & Greta Schiller.
96 pp., 25 illus. ISBN 0-941483-20-7   7.95

WE WALK THE BACK OF THE TIGER by Patricia A. Murphy.
192 pp. Romantic Lesbian novel/beginning women's movement.
ISBN 0-941483-13-4   8.95

SUNDAY'S CHILD by Joyce Bright. 216 pp. Lesbian athletics, at
last the novel about sports. ISBN 0-941483-12-6   8.95

OSTEN'S BAY by Zenobia N. Vole. 204 pp. Sizzling adventure
romance set on Bonaire. ISBN 0-941483-15-0   8.95

LESSONS IN MURDER by Claire McNab. 216 pp. 1st Det. Inspec.
Carol Ashton mystery — erotic tension!. ISBN 0-941483-14-2   8.95

YELLOWTHROAT by Penny Hayes. 240 pp. Margarita, bandit,
kidnaps Julia. ISBN 0-941483-10-X   8.95

SAPPHISTRY: THE BOOK OF LESBIAN SEXUALITY by
Pat Califia. 3d edition, revised. 208 pp. ISBN 0-941483-24-X   8.95

CHERISHED LOVE by Evelyn Kennedy. 192 pp. Erotic
Lesbian love story. ISBN 0-941483-08-8   8.95

LAST SEPTEMBER by Helen R. Hull. 208 pp. Six stories & a
glorious novella. ISBN 0-941483-09-6   8.95

THE SECRET IN THE BIRD by Camarin Grae. 312 pp. Striking,
psychological suspense novel. ISBN 0-941483-05-3   8.95

TO THE LIGHTNING by Catherine Ennis. 208 pp. Romantic
Lesbian 'Robinson Crusoe' adventure. ISBN 0-941483-06-1   8.95

THE OTHER SIDE OF VENUS by Shirley Verel. 224 pp.
Luminous, romantic love story. ISBN 0-941483-07-X   8.95

DREAMS AND SWORDS by Katherine V. Forrest. 192 pp.
Romantic, erotic, imaginative stories. ISBN 0-941483-03-7   8.95

MEMORY BOARD by Jane Rule. 336 pp. Memorable novel
about an aging Lesbian couple. ISBN 0-941483-02-9   9.95

THE ALWAYS ANONYMOUS BEAST by Lauren Wright
Douglas. 224 pp. A Caitlin Reese mystery. First in a series.
ISBN 0-941483-04-5   8.95

SEARCHING FOR SPRING by Patricia A. Murphy. 224 pp.
Novel about the recovery of love. ISBN 0-941483-00-2   8.95

DUSTY'S QUEEN OF HEARTS DINER by Lee Lynch. 240 pp.
Romantic blue-collar novel. ISBN 0-941483-01-0   8.95

PARENTS MATTER by Ann Muller. 240 pp. Parents'
relationships with Lesbian daughters and gay sons.
ISBN 0-930044-91-6   9.95

THE PEARLS by Shelley Smith. 176 pp. Passion and fun in
the Caribbean sun.   ISBN 0-930044-93-2   7.95

MAGDALENA by Sarah Aldridge. 352 pp. Epic Lesbian novel
set on three continents.   ISBN 0-930044-99-1   8.95

THE BLACK AND WHITE OF IT by Ann Allen Shockley.
144 pp. Short stories.   ISBN 0-930044-96-7   7.95

SAY JESUS AND COME TO ME by Ann Allen Shockley. 288
pp. Contemporary romance.   ISBN 0-930044-98-3   8.95

LOVING HER by Ann Allen Shockley. 192 pp. Romantic love
story.   ISBN 0-930044-97-5   7.95

MURDER AT THE NIGHTWOOD BAR by Katherine V.
Forrest. 240 pp. A Kate Delafield mystery. Second in a series.
                                      ISBN 0-930044-92-4   8.95

ZOE'S BOOK by Gail Pass. 224 pp. Passionate, obsessive love
story.   ISBN 0-930044-95-9   7.95

WINGED DANCER by Camarin Grae. 228 pp. Erotic Lesbian
adventure story.   ISBN 0-930044-88-6   8.95

PAZ by Camarin Grae. 336 pp. Romantic Lesbian adventurer
with the power to change the world.   ISBN 0-930044-89-4   8.95

SOUL SNATCHER by Camarin Grae. 224 pp. A puzzle, an
adventure, a mystery — Lesbian romance.   ISBN 0-930044-90-8   8.95

THE LOVE OF GOOD WOMEN by Isabel Miller. 224 pp.
Long-awaited new novel by the author of the beloved *Patience
and Sarah.*   ISBN 0-930044-81-9   8.95

THE HOUSE AT PELHAM FALLS by Brenda Weathers. 240
pp. Suspenseful Lesbian ghost story. ISBN 0-930044-79-7   7.95

HOME IN YOUR HANDS by Lee Lynch. 240 pp. More stories
from the author of *Old Dyke Tales.* ISBN 0-930044-80-0   7.95

EACH HAND A MAP by Anita Skeen. 112 pp. Real-life poems
that touch us all.   ISBN 0-930044-82-7   6.95

SURPLUS by Sylvia Stevenson. 342 pp. A classic early Lesbian
novel.   ISBN 0-930044-78-9   7.95

PEMBROKE PARK by Michelle Martin. 256 pp. Derring-do
and daring romance in Regency England.   ISBN 0-930044-77-0   7.95

THE LONG TRAIL by Penny Hayes. 248 pp. Vivid adventures
of two women in love in the old west.   ISBN 0-930044-76-2   8.95

HORIZON OF THE HEART by Shelley Smith. 192 pp. Hot
romance in summertime New England.   ISBN 0-930044-75-4   7.95

AN EMERGENCE OF GREEN by Katherine V. Forrest. 288
pp. Powerful novel of sexual discovery.   ISBN 0-930044-69-X   8.95

THE LESBIAN PERIODICALS INDEX edited by Claire
Potter. 432 pp. Author & subject index.   ISBN 0-930044-74-6   29.95

DESERT OF THE HEART by Jane Rule. 224 pp. A classic;
basis for the movie *Desert Hearts.*   ISBN 0-930044-73-8   7.95

SPRING FORWARD/FALL BACK by Sheila Ortiz Taylor.
288 pp. Literary novel of timeless love.   ISBN 0-930044-70-3   7.95

FOR KEEPS by Elisabeth Nonas. 144 pp. Contemporary novel
about losing and finding love.   ISBN 0-930044-71-1   7.95

TORCHLIGHT TO VALHALLA by Gale Wilhelm. 128 pp.
Classic novel by a great Lesbian writer.   ISBN 0-930044-68-1   7.95

LESBIAN NUNS: BREAKING SILENCE edited by Rosemary
Curb and Nancy Manahan. 432 pp. Unprecedented autobiographies
of religious life.   ISBN 0-930044-62-2   9.95

THE SWASHBUCKLER by Lee Lynch. 288 pp. Colorful novel
set in Greenwich Village in the sixties.   ISBN 0-930044-66-5   8.95

MISFORTUNE'S FRIEND by Sarah Aldridge. 320 pp. Histori-
cal Lesbian novel set on two continents.   ISBN 0-930044-67-3   7.95

A STUDIO OF ONE'S OWN by Ann Stokes. Edited by
Dolores Klaich. 128 pp. Autobiography.   ISBN 0-930044-64-9   7.95

SEX VARIANT WOMEN IN LITERATURE by Jeannette
Howard Foster. 448 pp. Literary history.   ISBN 0-930044-65-7   8.95

A HOT-EYED MODERATE by Jane Rule. 252 pp. Hard-hitting
essays on gay life; writing; art.   ISBN 0-930044-57-6   7.95

INLAND PASSAGE AND OTHER STORIES by Jane Rule.
288 pp. Wide-ranging new collection.   ISBN 0-930044-56-8   7.95

WE TOO ARE DRIFTING by Gale Wilhelm. 128 pp. Timeless
Lesbian novel, a masterpiece.   ISBN 0-930044-61-4   6.95

AMATEUR CITY by Katherine V. Forrest. 224 pp. A Kate
Delafield mystery. First in a series.   ISBN 0-930044-55-X   8.95

THE SOPHIE HOROWITZ STORY by Sarah Schulman. 176
pp. Engaging novel of madcap intrigue.   ISBN 0-930044-54-1   7.95

THE BURNTON WIDOWS by Vickie P. McConnell. 272 pp. A
Nyla Wade mystery, second in the series.   ISBN 0-930044-52-5   7.95

OLD DYKE TALES by Lee Lynch. 224 pp. Extraordinary
stories of our diverse Lesbian lives.   ISBN 0-930044-51-7   8.95

DAUGHTERS OF A CORAL DAWN by Katherine V. Forrest.
240 pp. Novel set in a Lesbian new world.   ISBN 0-930044-50-9   8.95

THE PRICE OF SALT by Claire Morgan. 288 pp. A milestone
novel, a beloved classic.   ISBN 0-930044-49-5   8.95

AGAINST THE SEASON by Jane Rule. 224 pp. Luminous,
complex novel of interrelationships.   ISBN 0-930044-48-7   8.95

LOVERS IN THE PRESENT AFTERNOON by Kathleen
Fleming. 288 pp. A novel about recovery and growth.
        ISBN 0-930044-46-0   8.95

TOOTHPICK HOUSE by Lee Lynch. 264 pp. Love between
two Lesbians of different classes.   ISBN 0-930044-45-2   7.95

MADAME AURORA by Sarah Aldridge. 256 pp. Historical
novel featuring a charismatic "seer."   ISBN 0-930044-44-4   7.95

CURIOUS WINE by Katherine V. Forrest. 176 pp. Passionate
Lesbian love story, a best-seller.   ISBN 0-930044-43-6   8.95

BLACK LESBIAN IN WHITE AMERICA by Anita Cornwell.
141 pp. Stories, essays, autobiography.   ISBN 0-930044-41-X   7.95

CONTRACT WITH THE WORLD by Jane Rule. 340 pp.
Powerful, panoramic novel of gay life.   ISBN 0-930044-28-2   9.95

MRS. PORTER'S LETTER by Vicki P. McConnell. 224 pp.
The first Nyla Wade mystery.   ISBN 0-930044-29-0   7.95

TO THE CLEVELAND STATION by Carol Anne Douglas.
192 pp. Interracial Lesbian love story.   ISBN 0-930044-27-4   6.95

THE NESTING PLACE by Sarah Aldridge. 224 pp. A
three-woman triangle—love conquers all!   ISBN 0-930044-26-6   7.95

THIS IS NOT FOR YOU by Jane Rule. 284 pp. A letter to a
beloved is also an intricate novel.   ISBN 0-930044-25-8   8.95

FAULTLINE by Sheila Ortiz Taylor. 140 pp. Warm, funny,
literate story of a startling family.   ISBN 0-930044-24-X   6.95

THE LESBIAN IN LITERATURE by Barbara Grier. 3d ed.
Foreword by Maida Tilchen. 240 pp. Comprehensive bibliography.
Literary ratings; rare photos.   ISBN 0-930044-23-1   7.95

ANNA'S COUNTRY by Elizabeth Lang. 208 pp. A woman
finds her Lesbian identity.   ISBN 0-930044-19-3   6.95

PRISM by Valerie Taylor. 158 pp. A love affair between two
women in their sixties.   ISBN 0-930044-18-5   6.95

BLACK LESBIANS: AN ANNOTATED BIBLIOGRAPHY
compiled by J. R. Roberts. Foreword by Barbara Smith. 112 pp.
Award-winning bibliography.   ISBN 0-930044-21-5   5.95

THE MARQUISE AND THE NOVICE by Victoria Ramstetter.
108 pp. A Lesbian Gothic novel.   ISBN 0-930044-16-9   6.95

OUTLANDER by Jane Rule. 207 pp. Short stories and essays
by one of our finest writers.   ISBN 0-930044-17-7   8.95

ALL TRUE LOVERS by Sarah Aldridge. 292 pp. Romantic
novel set in the 1930s and 1940s.   ISBN 0-930044-10-X   7.95

A WOMAN APPEARED TO ME by Renee Vivien. 65 pp. A
classic; translated by Jeannette H. Foster.   ISBN 0-930044-06-1   5.00

CYTHEREA'S BREATH by Sarah Aldridge. 240 pp. Romantic
novel about women's entrance into medicine.
        ISBN 0-930044-02-9   6.95

TOTTIE by Sarah Aldridge. 181 pp. Lesbian romance in the
turmoil of the sixties.   ISBN 0-930044-01-0   6.95
THE LATECOMER by Sarah Aldridge. 107 pp. A delicate love
story.   ISBN 0-930044-00-2   6.95

ODD GIRL OUT by Ann Bannon.   ISBN 0-930044-83-5   5.95
I AM A WOMAN by Ann Bannon.   ISBN 0-930044-84-3   5.95
WOMEN IN THE SHADOWS by Ann Bannon.
                                     ISBN 0-930044-85-1   5.95
JOURNEY TO A WOMAN by Ann Bannon.
                                     ISBN 0-930044-86-X   5.95
BEEBO BRINKER by Ann Bannon.   ISBN 0-930044-87-8   5.95
            Legendary novels written in the fifties and sixties,
               set in the gay mecca of Greenwich Village.

VOLUTE BOOKS

JOURNEY TO FULFILLMENT   Early classics by Valerie   3.95
A WORLD WITHOUT MEN   Taylor: The Erika Frohmann   3.95
RETURN TO LESBOS   series.   3.95

These are just a few of the many Naiad Press titles — we are the oldest and
largest lesbian/feminist publishing company in the world. Please request a
complete catalog. We offer personal service; we encourage and welcome
direct mail orders from individuals who have limited access to bookstores
carrying our publications.